"You mean you take all this seriously?"

Roz's voice rose from its normally controlled tones to an outraged squeal.

"Certainly." Charles seemed rather amused. "It might be all a game to you, but I don't play that sort of game. When I play, I play for keeps." The amusement was gone, and he sounded grimly resolved.

"I've drafted a notice for the papers, the usual thing: 'A marriage has been arranged...and will take place...' and I shall send it in as soon as I've applied for the license and made arrangements with the registrar. It's high time you were wedded and bedded. You're lethal running around loose."

His smile as he looked at her was distinctly wolfish. She'd have to tread very carefully to get out of this mess without a husband....

Tame a
Proud Heart

Jeneth Murrey

Harlequin Books

TORONTO • NEW YORK • LOS ANGELES • LONDON
AMSTERDAM • PARIS • SYDNEY • HAMBURG
STOCKHOLM • ATHENS • TOKYO • MILAN

Original hardcover edition published in 1982
by Mills & Boon Limited

ISBN 0-373-02559-9

Harlequin Romance first edition July 1983

CHAPTER ONE

'Isn't he beautiful, Roz, and wasn't he worth all the trouble?' Eve Berry bent over the sleeping baby in her arms and carefully wiped his milky mouth with a tissue. 'Yes, you are,' she informed him 'and you'd better start thanking your Aunty Roz for coming to the rescue. You're worth every day of that two months in bed before you were born and every minute of every day in bed since. But not to worry, my lad; I'm being allowed up in a few days' time and I'll soon have you outside in your pram. We'll go for lovely walks . . .' She raised her quiet, Madonna-like face with its wide blue eyes to her younger sister. 'He is lovely, isn't he, Roz? And I can never thank you enough, not if I live to be a hundred, for what you've done for us. Dropping everything at a moment's notice and coming down here when the alarm bells rang.'

Roz Wilshire smiled down at mother and son. 'Think nothing of it, just concentrate on getting well as soon as possible, because another week of my cooking and your husband is going to leave home!' She turned her head to catch a glimpse of herself and her sister in the dressing-table mirror. Two sisters with eight years between them; alike and yet unalike, it always fascinated her, the similarity and the difference.

Eve, the elder, looked like a Madonna, her fair hair parted in the middle and drawn back into

smooth waves which she tied with a piece of
ribbon or string or sometimes a rubber band,
whatever was handiest. There was a serene con-
tentment on her oval face, her eyes were quiet
and as blue as a summer sky and her mouth
curved with a secret pleasure.

Roz's own face was exactly the same shape as
her sister's and had she been plumper, had she
been filled with Eve's soul-deep content, they
would have been even more alike. But Roz's face
was more angular, the flesh more thinly spread so
that the bone structure showed through. Their
eyes were the same shape, long and thickly fringed
with dark lashes under dark, arched brows, but
hers lacked the blue softness of Eve's; they were a
clear, almost transparent grey which could darken
into storm when something disturbed her less
equable temperament. And her hair; there lay the
biggest difference; it was black and heavily
straight as though the weight of it pulled out any
tendency to curl or wave, but it grew back in the
same way and from the same broad forehead.

There were other differences in the sisters as
well, differences which weren't apparent while one
of them was in bed. Roz was two inches taller than
Eve and she lacked her sister's mature curves and
roundness. In their place was a long, slim, almost
nervous elegance so that she looked like a well-bred
racehorse which would bolt at the drop of a hat.

'I'll put him back in his cot now,' Roz offered,
'that's if you've finished cooing over him.'

Eve handed over her son reluctantly, her fingers
lingering on him, twitching his clothing into position and stroking the soft roundness of his cheeks.

Then when she finally released him, she sat back against her pillows, fiddling with the empty feeding bottle.

'I loathe this,' she snapped at the rubber teat, pulling it viciously between her fingers. 'I fed the two girls myself and it was much better, much more convenient as well. I felt better doing it that way and I *liked* it. What pleasure is there in knowing he's had so many ounces of dried-up, defatted cow-juice dissolved in water?' Her mouth drooped, losing its contented curve so that she looked almost sullen. 'He's a perfectly normal baby and I could have fed him normally without any of this rotten palaver of measuring things out and sterilising everything in sight!'

Roz tucked the baby into his cot and came back to the bedside with a bowl of water and a soapy sponge. 'You know why, darling. Your little op— it upset things . . .'

Eve's face flushed with indignation. 'My little op! Damn those busybody doctors, and damn Stephen as well for letting them do it to me. He had no right . . . Both of you took advantage of the fact that I wasn't in any condition to stand up for myself, and now I've been neutered, or whatever it is they do. Oh!' she screwed up her eyes and squealed with fury. 'I *like* babies, I adore them, and I intended to have another whether the doctors said it was wise or not. They aren't all that clever, you know, they said I couldn't have this one, and they were wrong!'

Roz knew better than to argue. When her normally placid sister became steamed up about something, it was better to stay quiet until the kettle went off the boil, so to speak. Instead, she became placating. 'See what I mean, darling?' she pointed out gently. 'You're in a highly nervous state, not at all like my beautiful, calm sister. And do stop saying "neutered" as though you were a tomcat! It's not like that at all and you know it.'

'And it won't make any difference to me?' Eve's mouth twisted into a sarcastic, disbelieving curve. 'I don't believe it, I never did. That's one reason why I was so against it, and Stephen agreed with me. He promised me he wouldn't allow them to do it, and then, when it came to the crunch, he signed me away like a lamb. He let them carve me up!'

'I don't think he had much choice,' Roz continued to soothe. 'Stephen's a Professor of English, love. He'd be the first to admit he doesn't know a damn thing about medicine or anatomy. And what's more, you're a big girl now, nearly thirty-four, which is quite old enough to realise the doctors wouldn't have recommended something if they didn't think it was in your best interests.'

'I told Stephen I thought it might interfere with our relationship, our married life, and he agreed with me.' Eve was still mutinous. 'I made him promise he wouldn't allow . . .'

'Eve, stop harping on about it,' Roz sighed. 'Forget it! Concentrate on your baby and getting well.'

'Mmm.' But Eve couldn't abandon it, her face broke into a sad smile as she looked towards the cot. 'Oh, but doesn't it make you want to weep, Roz? To think I'll never have another baby!'

'You have three already.' Roz tried to be firm and bracing, to inject a little humour so that her sister's gloom would vanish. 'According to the statistics, Mrs Average only has two and a half babies; you see, you've had more than your share. It's all pure melodrama, carrying on like this, and you know it. Now may I go, please, I've things to do.'

Eve clutched at her hand. 'Forgive me, darling. I've been quite abominable, haven't I? And after all you've done for us. Yes, you have,' she stifled Roz's protest. 'You've been here with me for nearly three months, and your career's in tatters.'

'Some career!' Roz snorted delicately down her small, straight nose as she straightened the bed and plumped up the pillows. 'If I'd been a teacher, as I always wanted to be, I'd allow you that remark. Being a photographic model can't be classed as a career, I only went into it after I'd been turned down by every education authority in the country. To most people, my kind of work counts as a shady pastime; besides, I've been doing it now for five years with varying degrees of success, so it's about time I had a change, don't you think?'

'A change?' Eve squeaked with excitement.

'Mmm,' Roz collected the baby impedimenta on to a tray. 'I've had a couple of other offers . . .'

'Tell me . . .'

'No,' Roz was firm. 'You have a little nap first, then eat your lunch without telling me what I've done wrong with it; take your pills without yelling that they're big enough to choke a horse and I'll . . . Oh, Lord, will you listen to that!' She broke off as yells of thwarted fury reverberated through the house. 'Gilly!'

'Bring her in here,' Eve directed. 'My son is asleep and she'll lie down beside me and snooze for an hour—we'll all snooze!'

Roz dropped the tray to speed out of the room and returned a few moments later with a wriggling three-year-old who was heaving gusty sobs. 'A real demolition expert,' Roz chuckled. 'I don't think that playpen will ever be the same again.'

'Darling!' Eve cooed, and the tears and sobs ceased, to be replaced by a wide satisfied smile. 'All right, Roz, you can leave her with me, we'll all have a nice nap.'

Roz sped downstairs swiftly. From the dining room she could hear the whine of a vacuum cleaner; the daily woman was doing her bit! But Roz's goal was the kitchen where she had a lamb casserole in the oven, a casserole prepared strictly according to the book, so if there was anything wrong with it, it wasn't her fault. She opened the oven door an inch or so and sniffed cautiously. It smelled all right but . . . Then she firmly crushed down the desire to take the dish out and prod it about a bit, instead busying herself with putting the baby's bottles in the sterilizer and tidying up the little mess she'd made before she sat down at the kitchen table to re-read the two letters which had come by that morning's post. She sat holding them, one in either hand, and weighing them as if the heaviness of the paper would have some influence on her choice and she choked back a small flare of annoyance when Stephen, her brother-in-law, walked in to disturb her thoughts. She set

her face into a cool, smiling mask and was icily
polite.

'Good morning, Stephen, and what can I do
for you?'

'Roz.' His deep voice was husky and his great
size seemed to fill the room. Idly she noticed that
despite the salads and other parts of his careful
dict, he was putting on weight. He was broader,
more massive than when she had first known him
seven years ago. He hadn't been a Professor then,
just the senior lecturer in English, a big, golden
god of a man; like a Viking with his red gold hair
and beard and his sea-blue eyes.

And she, a starry-eyed nineteen, had fallen flat
on her face, worshipping before him and hanging
avidly on every word which fell from his lips. Not
that she'd been alone in doing this, oh no!
Practically every other girl in the faculty was in
the same boat with her, they would all have laid
themselves down flat to make a carpet for him to
walk on. But she had been lucky; they, the girls,
all told her so; she had so much more than a warm,
understanding smile and a kind, encouraging
word. She had Stephen's arms about her and his
deep voice murmuring things about twin souls in
her ear. Life had been big and golden, like
Stephen, and she had floated along on a sea of
bliss, making the most supreme idiot of herself.

And then she had taken him home for the
weekend; her parents were dead and there was
just Eve, running the house, and Eve had made
him welcome. He'd come on a lot of weekends
and had ended up marrying Eve. Loving her elder
sister as she did, Roz had forgiven him that, but

what she could never forgive was that he'd been making love to Eve and flirting gently with herself at the same time. It disillusioned her, and she came out of her romantic daydream cynically certain that men were some low form of life and that none of them could be trusted as far as they could be thrown.

Even then, she had managed to be composed, to hide her heartbreak beneath a smile and to enter into Eve's joy, because Eve had never realised how strong had been her love for Stephen and Roz was so ashamed of herself that she vowed Eve should never know.

Roz hadn't lost her head, somewhere inside her was a strip of tempered steel which wouldn't allow her to bend or break. She'd been grimly practical; smiling all through the wedding and the lengthy reception which followed it and then going back to college and sweating her way through her last year and the final exams at the end of it. Hers hadn't been a very good degree, but then it couldn't be expected that a girl whose heart had been broken would get a First.

And for seven years she had managed to maintain the warmth which had always existed between herself and her sister without indulging in very much close contact; that was, up until three months ago when Eve had sent out her S.O.S. and she had come hotfoot back to this sleepy little Sussex village, taken one look at Stephen and the scales had fallen from her eyes.

She had come when Eve called, quiet and calm on the surface as she had trained herself to appear, and at last she realised that she had wasted—that was the only word for it, wasted—seven long years in mourning for a man who either had never existed except in her imagination, or who didn't exist any longer. Roz wondered where her golden god had gone because there was nothing now but a well preserved man in his early forties, but unfortunately, a man who was used to admiration, who expected it as his due; who expected her to be the same as in the old days. The god had existed only in her imagination and she had kept the memory fresh all these years only to find that he was nothing, nothing at all.

She hadn't said any of this, not in so many words, but she'd done her best to make it clear. It was then that she discovered that Stephen was not only a well preserved forty odd, a Professor of English, a husband to Eve and a father to three children, he was conceited, blind and stupid into the bargain. He actually expected her to start worshipping again! He was being stupid now, at this moment, speaking in tones of husky intimacy as though they shared some wonderful secret. It made her angry, not so much with him as with her own adolescent idiocy.

'Roz,' his voice came again, demanding attention, and she pushed the letters back into the pocket of her skirt and turned a bright smile on him.

'Have you been up to see Eve and the baby?' She made it sound as bright as her smile and as impersonal and she dragged the letters from her pocket once more and made a great thing of re-reading one of them, although she already knew it off by heart.

'Not yet. I wanted to see you first.' He smiled at her conspiratorially.

'Good,' Roz smiled at him blandly, 'because I wanted to see you. I'm going up to London on—er—Friday,' she consulted the letter again, 'and I may not be able to get back the same day. Eve will be up by then, but I'd like you to arrange with the daily woman to be here with her. She'll try to do too much, and we don't want her having a relapse, do we?'

'I'll see to it,' he promised, and then, 'What's the matter, Roz?'

'The matter?' She raised her eyebrows fractionally. 'I don't know what you mean. There's nothing the matter with me.'

'You're so different,' he sounded mournful. 'Not at all like the girl I used to know.'

'Seven years makes a difference,' she pointed out hardily.

'But we shared so much in the old days . . .'

'We shared very little,' she cut in curtly. 'I sat at your feet and worshipped, that was all. A bad case of teenage infatuation, like measles or mumps. We all get it and we all get over it. You should know that, Stephen.'

'Oh, I think it was more than that,' he smiled down at her confidently, a radiant smile which lit up his sea blue eyes. 'Let me not to the marriage of true minds admit impediment,' he quoted sententiously.

'Oh, my mind,' her mouth curved in amusement. 'You mean you were interested in my *mind*!'

'I still am, Roz, my dear. A brilliant mind, one

I could have moulded, developed . . .'

Hastily she controlled her snort of derisive laughter. It was one thing which she had learned in the past three months; Stephen couldn't bear being laughed at, it turned his golden camaraderie into something small and ugly.

'We're wandering away from the main issue,' she interrupted. 'I'd be more grateful if you could work up a little interest in Eve's mind. She's feeling very low and she's doing a very good job of convincing herself that she's for evermore useless as a wife. She needs reassurance, and you're the only one who can give it to her. This lecture tour you've got lined up for the summer vacation, is it really necessary?'

'The organisers have been in touch with me this morning,' he sounded obstinate and vaguely sulky. 'The halls have been booked, tickets have already been sold; my lectures are very popular, you know.'

'And you mustn't disappoint your adoring public,' she said bitterly. 'It doesn't matter about Eve and the children as long as those American matrons aren't disappointed!'

'Eve wants me to go.' He came round the table to lay a hand on her shoulder, and she flinched away from his touch.

'Then that's all right and I won't interfere any more,' she glared up at him, 'but I think you've got your priorities wrong, and since this is a free country and Eve's my only sister, I think I'm entitled to say so. Now, I suggest you pop upstairs and have a word with her—it's all quiet and peaceful. You won't have a chance this afternoon when Freda comes home from school,' and she turned her attention back to the letter in her hand.

'A love letter?' He was heavy-handed in his teasing.

'No,' she returned calmly. 'An offer of a job, and I must answer it straight away, so if you'll excuse me . . .' she twisted her face into a remote, meaningless smile. 'Lunch will be ready at one, it's a lamb casserole, so if you want something different, you'd better let me know.'

When Stephen had gone, she returned her attention back to the letters. One of them was an offer of a post as fashion buyer in a big London store; the other was from a monthly magazine and looked much more interesting. The editor wanted her to do a series of articles on fashion and beauty, one a month for a year, and she rather liked the idea. After all, she'd had five years as a human clothes peg and it had taught her a lot. She counted herself something of an expert when it came to clothes and make-up.

It didn't take her long to make up her mind. The magazine won; fashion buying was a chancy business. She could so easily make a mistake, go for a line which didn't 'take'. No, she'd accept the magazine's offer, and she swiftly wrote the editor a short note to say she was interested in the offer and would be in town on Friday and would call in to discuss it.

At three o'clock, she walked down to the village and posted her letter, watching the envelope slip through the slot with a feeling of satisfaction. At last she would be out of the rat race, a race where there were always dozens of young, nubile girls willing and ready to step into her shoes. At twenty-five, nearly twenty-six, she thought she was getting a bit too old for close-up photography, and in any case, she was bored with it. There must be something better in life than constantly smiling into a camera!

At four o'clock, Freda, her elder niece, hopped off the school bus and claimed her attention. 'Has Mummy still got that baby?' she demanded.

'It's a permanent fixture, I'm afraid,' Roz grinned down at Freda's solemn little face. 'Like you asked, I had a word with the doctor, but he says there's no chance of sending it back. You'll just have to grin and bear it,' and she clasped Freda's six-year-old, rather grubby hand in her own and together they walked down the little side road which led to the house, Freda explaining as they went that she had no rooted objection to babies in general but that she would have preferred another sister. School had taught her that boys were noisy, rough creatures who, when they weren't playing football, pulled pigtails and made rude noises.

Roz comforted the little girl with the promise of baked beans on toast for tea, followed by apple tart and cream and the thought that when her baby brother was old enough to play football and pull pigtails she, Freda, would be too big to be bothered with such infantile pastimes.

Stephen had forgotten to approach the daily woman with the request for a full day's attendance on Friday, so Roz had to arrange it herself, and it was more difficult than she had imagined. The daily woman 'couldn't,' she had her other ladies to consider, but eventually she thought of somebody who 'could' and who'd be glad of the money. Roz was to travel up by train and return either late on Friday night or on Saturday, depending on how long her business took.

'But you promise to come back!' Eve clutched at her sister's hand and then let go of it swiftly. 'Sorry Roz. I've grown so used to your being here again, but I shouldn't cling, should I?'

'Certainly I'll be back,' Roz soothed. 'It's only an interview, they aren't going to lock me in an office, you know. In any case, those things which can be done to prepare the British female for her summer holidays have already been done. I should think I'll probably start in September, telling those same British females how to get into shape for Christmas.'

'You could work from here,' Eve mused aloud. 'Think how lovely that would be, just like the old days before you went up to university.'

Roz didn't think it would be lovely, she didn't think it would be wise either. Her naturally quick mind examined that possible future, weighed it up and discarded it swiftly, but she was wise enough not to say so. 'We'll see,' she was comfortably encouraging.

In London she found her editor, a charming woman who patiently explained what would be required of her but who was remarkably firm on the subject of what the magazine wanted.

'We'll need a few more photographs. These,' she tapped Roz's portfolio, 'I'm afraid they won't do.'

Roz raised her eyebrows. 'Won't do? What's wrong with them, they're all very recent.'

'Wrong image,' the editor was firm again. 'They're much too glamorous. All right, I daresay, for an advertiser, but for your articles we'll need something much more approachable, somebody our readers can identify with. You know what I mean; we want less of a fashion mask, more of a woman. Somebody who will understand and sympathise, somebody they can write to for help. Honestly, if you didn't know what to do to make yourself look better, would you ask her?' She tossed over a black and white glossy, and Roz examined herself for the first time in years.

There was sophistication there, and an utter lack of humanity; the face was like a stylised portrait painted on a smooth oval. She shuddered slightly and pushed the photograph back. So this was what she had become! She was glad she was getting out of it. While she was thinking this, she heard the editor's voice as from a distance.

'We've made an appointment for you with Charles for tomorrow morning at ten. We've told him what we want and as you've worked with him before, you know you can safely leave it all in his hands. I've made a note of the address for you, although I suppose you don't really need it; you must know your way there blindfold. Will that be convenient for you, because if not . . .'

'No, it'll be quite convenient,' Roz gave a little smile. 'I can go back to Sussex tomorrow evening or even Sunday.'

Roz took a taxi back to the small hotel where she was staying, bought a couple of paperbacks in a nearby newsagent's, ate her dinner and went to her room intending to read, but the books held no appeal. As if it was some sort of talisman, she constantly fingered the piece of paper on which Charles' name and address was typed. As her editor had said, she didn't need it, she knew it already, by heart. It was where her agent had sent her when she had first come to London and she had been going to him in the course of her work for five years. If one could ever think of a photographer's studio as home, Charles' was hers.

She had been new to the job then, and her agent had dismissed her portfolio of photographs with a wave of his hand and a look of contempt. 'Too provincial,' he had explained. 'They're not bad, but I want something better. Make an appointment with Charles—Charles Maine, here's the address.'

But tomorrow wouldn't be like that first time she had gone to him, she grinned at herself as her mind slipped back to that time. There had been an agonising week's wait before she could be fitted in and then she had to get past his secretary, no easy thing, because the secretary was sophisticatedly efficient and had frightened Roz into a fit of trembling. She had walked up the stairs on shaking legs and into the big, bare studio at the top of the house. She had been conscious of a feeling of disappointment when she had first seen him, although she hadn't known really what she was expecting.

'Miss Roz Wilshire?' He had come towards her, well over medium height but short of Stephen's towering magnificence. A slender, dark man, his hair unfashionably short with one lock falling over his high forehead. His face, she decided, wasn't moulded, it was hewn out of something hard and durable, and it was expressionless, only his eyes were alive. Dark, shrewd eyes which looked at her, dismantled her into her separate component parts, evaluated each and then had put her together again carelessly.

He had called her 'darling', but so did every other photographer she had ever worked with. She thought it was because none of them could remember names, only faces; it seemed to be a standard form of address, but for all that, his way of working was completely different. There was no frantic clicking of the shutter, not then or at any time later. Charles came towards her, gripped her chin firmly in his fingers and turned her face to the light.

'Go and wash it off, darling!' He had sounded weary. 'Take off that muck on your eyes and wipe away that ghastly lipstick. Minimum make-up, blusher here and here,' he traced the areas with a careless finger. 'Not too much eyeliner, a paler lipstick and only a little gloss right at the centre.' And he had pushed her in the direction of a small washroom. 'Five minutes,' he had warned, and then he had apparently forgotten all about her.

Roz had felt vaguely humiliated, like a small child who had been caught playing with her mother's cosmetics, but she had done as she had been told so that when she had emerged from the washroom, all her sophistication was gone and she was just a good-looking girl with wide eyes and a soft, pink, generous mouth.

Charles had nodded his approval of the transformation, tilted her chin again in his fingers, said, 'Twelve o'clock high,' to the boy with the lights and they had started work. After about a quarter of an hour Charles had abandoned his camera and advanced on her.

'Are you wearing falsies?' he had demanded.

Roz had felt herself colour all over with embarrassment. 'No!'

'Then take off that damn bra, it spoils the line,' and once more he directed her to the washroom. As she went, he called after her, 'The place for breasts is where yours are,' and she turned to find him grinning at her derisively. 'And they're a nice size, so there's no need for you to drag them up underneath your chin.'

Roz had crept away from the studio that day feeling humiliated, but those pictures had started her career. They had also started a rather bitter friendship with Charles, a pin-pricking relationship. He was a marvellous photographer and he made the most of her; he had even taken her out to dinner occasionally. 'Good for your image,' he had explained sardonically. There was a magnetism about him, a strange magic, because he wasn't all that good-looking or good-tempered either. But Roz was off good looks and good temper; Stephen had put her off. Even so, Charles got through to her sometimes so that, if she wasn't careful, she found herself nearly doing what he wanted.

She liked to think of Charles as a friend, but Charles didn't wish to be thought of as friendly.

He had his sights set on a much warmer and deeper relationship, and this had upset her. Somehow the thought of herself, Charles and a temporary affair had jarred. She wasn't the type for affairs anyway.

His studio was in some mews behind Church Street and she made her way there on Saturday morning, arranging it so that she was dead on time. Charles loathed waiting for anybody. It was a hidden, quiet little street, difficult to find, as though he shunned publicity, as though he preferred to be apart from the crowd, a lone wolf. Roz grinned to herself; no, not a wolf, just a very choosy cat that walked by itself. The place was probably described as a 'mews cottage', but it wasn't Roz's idea of a cottage. Upstairs was the studio, together with the darkroom and cubicle washrooms, but downstairs elegance reigned. That was where Charles lived, and he was a stickler for elegance and perfection.

Today, there was no secretary to bar her way and Charles met her at the studio door. 'I've to humanise you, darling. Take away the magic, remove that "untouchable" look.'

She smiled at him. 'Will it be very difficult? I've brought some other clothes with me if you'd rather . . .'

He eyed the striped silk shirt which she was wearing and the gently flared, grey flannel skirt. 'No, I don't think so. Those are country type clothes, they'll do nicely. Take off your jacket and undo the top button of the shirt, otherwise you'll look like a schoolmarm. We won't bother about the rest today, not until we see how this lot turns out.'

CHAPTER TWO

THE photographic session lasted for a good two hours, and at the end of it Roz's 'sympathetic' smile felt like a death's head grin; her shoulders had stiffened and there was a nagging pain in the back of her neck. Charles came behind her where she sat, his thin, strong fingers finding the spot and massaging expertly until the hard knot of tension softened. Unaccountably, she shivered at his touch.

'Tell me about it,' he suggested.

'Tell you what?' She turned her head and winced; the pain wasn't so bad, but it was still there. 'There's nothing to tell.'

'No?' He came round in front of her and tilted her chin to look down at her with wry amusement. 'The first time you ever came here, you were as nervous as a cat, but you refused to let it show. I admired you for that, because I'd not have known except for your fingers which kept clenching into claws. But today it's different. You're putting on a good show and your hands are under control, but the tension's showing through. You aren't calm and serene any more. That's why your neck hurts and that's why I say "tell me about it".'

Roz moved away from him. Today, he was upsetting her just by looking and she felt safer with just a few feet between them. For something

to do, she stretched out for her jacket and began
to struggle herself into it.

'It's nothing,' she murmured. 'A bit of family trouble, that's all, it's nothing I can't
handle.'

'Mmm, I've noticed your absence—how long
is it, six months? For one mad, delirious
moment, I thought you were running away from
me.'

'Running away from you?' She summoned
up a look of wonder. 'Now why would I do
that?'

'Because I'd started to get through to you, darling. The last time we met I turned you on—and
don't bother to deny it, I wouldn't like to call a
lady a liar to her face.'

'So you did!' she grinned at him impertinently.
'But it was only a little bit, wasn't it? Nothing I
couldn't control. I'll start running away from you
when I get weak at the knees, and I'm not that far
gone yet.'

'Then I may still hope?' Charles grinned back
and started to unship the camera from its tripod,
handling the ugly, boxy-looking thing with almost
exaggerated care.

'The Hasselblad!' She made a face at him.
'Your treasured best in cameras! I'm honoured.
You've never used anything better than a Nikon
on me before.'

'Mmm, you are honoured—but stop trying to
change the subject. I'll allow you that three
months when you were doing that series of T.V.
commercials, but then you vanished from the face
of the earth. Where have you been, and what in

hell have you been doing with yourself—dieting?' While he was speaking, he had packed away the camera and come to sling a companionable arm about her waist and pressure her towards the stairs. Roz tried to turn back to retrieve her make-up case and the small holdall which contained her change of clothes, but the arm about her didn't slacken, it forced her willy-nilly down the stairs and into the neat, sunny little kitchen.

'Have some lunch,' Charles offered.

She was becoming angry, first with the way he was pulling and pushing her about and then by his altogether unexpected interest in her private affairs. 'I don't diet,' she informed him frostily, 'and I'm not at all hungry. Thank you for your kind offer, but I must get back.' That should have been the clinching line which would stop him in his tracks, but he paid no attention to it.

'No?' He smiled devastatingly and rattled about in the cutlery drawer, coming out with a handful of knives, forks and spoons. 'Here, set the table like a good girl while I see to the food.'

Roz accepted the cutlery with a bad grace and dumped it all on the table. 'I'm afraid I really can't spare the time,' she raised her nose several inches in the air. 'If I leave now, I could get a train back late this afternoon . . .'

'. . . And if you leave now, you might have to come up to town again next week,' Charles shrugged. 'It's entirely up to you. I tried for something special in those shots today and I shan't know if I've succeeded until I've seen the prints; which won't be until tomorrow at the earliest.'

'What happens if they're not up to standard?' Roz enquired. 'What should I have to do?'

'Make another appointment.' His dark eyes gleamed. 'But if you happened to be in town to-morrow, I would break the habit of a lifetime for you and work on Sunday. Suit yourself.'

'I could stay in town overnight,' she temporised, 'but all the same . . .'

'Make up your mind, sweetie, but if you're staying, you may as well sit down and eat. You say you haven't been dieting, but I estimate you've lost about seven pounds, and you can't afford it.' His eyes slid over her with a cruel light in their depths. 'If you were a teenager, it wouldn't matter, but you're—how old—twenty-six? You've started to look scraggy and haunted. You haven't noticed it yet and I don't suppose anybody else has, but I can see it, and the camera will pick it up.'

'Then you can expect scraggy and haunted prints, can't you?' She eyed him dourly. 'If I'm that bad, I wonder you bothered. Why are you getting at me?'

'Because, under your make-up and that bra which I told you not to wear, you're losing your looks. It used to be a pleasure to photograph you; I could take a print straight off the negative without going to a lot of trouble to make it look good. As you are now, I'll have to fog them a bit.'

'I like foggy prints,' she knew she was wriggling. 'Foggy, scraggy and haunted; it will add an air of mystery . . .'

'. . . And about ten years to your age,' Charles continued to be cruel.

She would have liked to tell him about it. She tried it out in her mind and it sounded awful, almost unbelievable. If it came from a teenager, it could be excused, but from herself at a more mature age; it wouldn't do. How could she say, 'I'm having trouble with my brother-in-law. I fell for him like a ton of bricks when I was nineteen, but he married my sister. Now he's starting to get ideas about me and I can't say anything because it would break my sister's heart, and I can't remove myself from the scene because I've promised Eve that I'll stay with her until she's better'?

No, she couldn't say any of those things; he'd probably laugh his head off, either that or be coldly cutting. It was all right for him, he could wield a surgeon's knife, tell her to get out and be damned to anybody; but he wasn't involved.

'So tell me,' he returned to the attack. 'If you refuse, I shall start making guesses. A man, I think, and probably married. Sit down and eat!' The last words came out with a sharp crack, like a shot from a gun as he fished in the microwave oven and came out with a large pie. 'Steak and kidney,' he informed her, 'and quite good.'

'You made it yourself, I suppose.' She was gently sarcastic, but the smell of it was making her mouth water and unconsciously she was grasping her knife and fork.

Charles cut the pie in half and slid one piece on to her plate. 'There's nothing to go with it, so don't scowl at the size of the portion. And no, Miss Smarty Pants, I didn't make it myself. As you know, I have a very efficient secretary/receptionist and she's a good cook. It's part of her duties to see that I don't starve.'

Roz ate slowly, savouring every mouthful; it was a very good pie. Of course, as she had pointed out, there was far too much for her, but with a slight surprise, she found herself chasing the last crumbs of pastry around the plate with her fork. Charles didn't speak while he was eating, so there was no need for her to think up polite conversation, she could be utterly relaxed and enjoy what she was eating, an enjoyment enhanced by the fact that she hadn't had such a filling or sustaining meal for a long time.

She was, after three months, heartily sick, of living in the small Sussex village and following the régime laid down by Stephen. She supposed that had Eve been able to get about, there would have been a greater variety and mealtimes would have been a little more interesting; she wasn't a bad cook herself, but Stephen was occupied with health and his waistline. All food was non-fattening, low in cholesterol, full of natural fibre and vitamins and free from artificial fertilisers; which meant that the evening meal usually consisted of thin slices of lean meat with a salad, on which Stephen would allow no dressing which contained oil. All bread was of the wholemeal variety and the meal always ended with yoghurt. Coffee, sugar and alcohol were out, since they all constituted a danger to health, being full of poison!

Roz would sit, watching Stephen champing on

lettuce while her temper rose. Salads were all right, but not *every* evening; she wanted, she dreamed of big, thick, juicy steaks with loads of French fries or buttered new potatoes, or better still, both. She liked her sweets to be fruity with lots of whipped cream and she longed for coffee, cups and cups of it, thick with cream and sweet with sugar. She had denied to Charles that she had been dieting, but it wasn't quite the truth; she was being dieted, and no amount of corned beef sandwiches, which was what she made for herself when she felt the pangs of hunger gnawing, made up for all the healthy food. She was beginning to believe that this was partly to blame for her unaccustomed meekness. She didn't usually suffer the pricks so tamely.

'Go into the lounge,' Charles suggested as he stirred himself to plug in the coffee machine. 'I'll bring this in when it's ready.'

The coffee seemed to take a long time to make. Roz curled up on the cushions of the divan and closed her eyes. There was a peace here which had nothing to do with there being no traffic noise—there wasn't any of that in Sussex; no, this peace was an intangible, fleeting thing which begged to be enjoyed, and she was enjoying it. When she opened her eyes again, evening shadows were everywhere, to set her blinking in disbelief.

'This man,' Charles' voice came out of the gloom, 'he's not only putting you off your food, he's giving you sleepless nights as well. If you want to stay in this game, sweetie, you'd better start getting over him.'

Roz was feeling better; she had eaten half an

enormous pie so that she had felt comfortably full, she had slept peacefully for a couple of hours with no interruptions and she was ready to fight.

'I told you, there's no man, not in the way you mean, but of course you won't believe that. Your mind is sex-orientated, and I suppose that's why you have this mad idea that I've been indulging in an immoral affair for the past three months.'

'Too much passion can make a girl thin,' he sounded bored. 'On the other hand, if you were fighting a battle with your conscience, that could do it as well.'

'And what do you propose?' she queried sarcastically. 'What cure do you recommend for this mythical lover of mine? The one who's either wearing me out or who I'm pining for.'

Charles smiled in the gloom, and perhaps it was a trick of the light, but she didn't like the quality of that smile. 'The cure for one man is another, darling; I was about to offer my services.'

'You!' She choked back an hysterical laugh 'You're mad, insane, you've lost your marbles!' Then she let a little of the laugh out and wished she hadn't; it was high, thin and creepy. 'You, the great Charles Maine! But you've hinted at this sort of thing before, haven't you, and surely you remember the answer that time. It was "no", and it hasn't changed. Besides, you've got your image and reputation to consider.'

'Mmm,' this time his smile was a real one. 'We could be discreet. As you say, I wouldn't like to damage my reputation.' She watched as he put aside the book which he'd been reading while she slept. He came across the room to sit beside her on the divan, and it was then that the funny side of it struck her so that she found herself stifling a giggle.

'Your reputation!' Her eyes twinkled. 'Charles, you haven't got one, at least not the sort anybody'd be worried about losing. For that, you'd have to be pure, and I don't think you could manage it. I've heard the most dreadful stories about your affairs, I'm told that they're pretty hectic but that they never last long and you always return to the arms of your secretary. The girl must be a saint, something very special.'

'You are so right, darling,' he shared her amusement. 'She is, very special.'

'Not to mention forgiving and broad-minded,' she chuckled. 'But what you're suggesting wouldn't do. I live in a little Sussex village where the mere holding of hands is considered to be a sign that the girl is weakening past the point of no return, and it's not the place to which you could bring your secretary.' She watched his mouth tighten and then relax as though she had hit a tender spot which he was quick to cover up.

'Why not? It's the first time anybody's suggested that my secretary isn't socially acceptable.'

'And I'm not suggesting it either.' Roz flushed with embarrassment. 'We're not snobs, but the villagers aren't what you'd call diplomatic, and they do love a good scandal; they'd embarrass the poor girl.'

'But don't you think she'd be rather superfluous?' His eyes gleamed and he deliberately turned the subject away from what she thought must be a private point of view. 'What is it you want to do? Bring this man up to scratch, discourage him completely, or would you rather I turned your thoughts into an entirely new channel, like this?' His arm came about her shoulders and his smooth dark head was lowered to hers. 'Just a sample of the wares on offer,' he murmured some time later as he lifted his mouth from hers.

Roz looked down at her hands while she tried to cope. What had started as an odd, quite pleasant joke wasn't a joke any longer, and she thought that 'pleasant' was a weak word to describe what she had just experienced. Charles had kissed her before, of course, or rather she had kissed Charles, as she had kissed quite a few men. She had always thought of it as a nice way of saying thank you for a pleasant dinner or an enjoyable evening's entertainment. Everybody kissed everybody nowadays, it meant no more than shaking hands, but this had been different. This was the first time she had been aware of enjoying it, the first time that she hadn't wanted it to stop.

Charles had not only kissed her thoroughly, he'd made her kiss him back, and he'd been very expert about it—although, as she realised with a sinking heart, such expertise didn't come from living a monastic existence. His mouth had been cool and firm on hers, he hadn't bruised her lips or slobbered and he had gentled her lips apart without force while his hand had slid down to her hips to pull her firmly against him. She felt his other hand now, warm on her back, exploring until his fingers hooked into elastic. He pulled and let the stretchy material snap back so that she yelped.

'I told you,' he was whispering it into the hollow behind her ear, 'you're better without that bra. Did you like the sample?'

Roz drew a deep breath and collected herself, forcing her voice to a cool, analytical tone. 'Too passionate!' She gave her verdict after a moment's consideration. 'I don't think you'd fit the bill, you're not sufficiently detached. And now, if you've finished playing games, I'll go. There's no way what you're offering would help me and there's no way I'd accept it. I don't go in much for emotional involvement; frigid, that's the word to describe me.'

His hands had slipped up to her shoulders and he was holding them firmly, his grip unrelaxing as he turned her to face him. 'You're a liar, darling. A beautiful one, but still a liar, and I've a good mind to teach you not to lie to me.'

'No,' she shook her head at him firmly. 'Like I said, you've got it all wrong. I'm having problems, who doesn't? But it's nothing to do with a man. It's my sister.' She made a vague gesture which dismissed Stephen as being only a minor source of trouble. 'It's all complicated stuff, families always are, but I can handle it easily, I assure you.'

'And you're lying through your teeth!' Charles sounded angry as though he couldn't bear to be wrong. 'You've got man trouble written all over you. Maybe you have a sister . . .'

'. . . I have!'

'. . . and maybe she is part of your worry, but the rest of it, my lovely, wears trousers and shaves every morning.'

'Not so.' Roz crossed her fingers although she was telling the truth. Stephen didn't shave, he only combed and trimmed his red-gold beard. She shrugged herself out of Charles' slackened grasp, swung her feet to the ground and stood up, smoothing her skirt down over her hips. 'Did I leave my things upstairs?'

'I brought them down here,' he nodded to where her small case and holdall stood by the door. 'And you're turning me down flat? Will you also turn down an invitation to dinner?'

'Mmm, flat!' she agreed with him, as she picked up her jacket and slipped her arms into the sleeves, disregarding his proffered help. She didn't want to touch him and she certainly didn't want him to touch her. Roz was a realist and honest enough to admit it when she came up against anything she couldn't handle. Just a few seconds ago, she had realised that she couldn't handle Charles. As she had often said, he was the cat which walked by himself, he was unpredictable and she didn't trust him. Or was it that she didn't trust herself?

Had she allowed him a few more minutes to continue with his cozening ways, she thought she would have been putty in those long, strong fingers; he'd have been able to do just what he wanted with her. She straightened her jacket, walked over to where her things were standing, picked them up and took a deep breath.

'I shan't be seeing you again, Charles. If I ever need another photograph, I'll find another photographer; one who doesn't have seduction in mind.'

'Seduction?' Charles looked innocent, or as innocent as it was possible for him to look. 'You've a depraved mind, darling, I was only offering to help.'

'The two words are synonymous where you're concerned,' she called over her shoulder, and went out, giving the door a hearty slam behind her.

Back at the small hotel, she ate dinner without much appetite and then retired to her room with the neglected paperbacks. They remained neglected, although one of them, thick and with an excitingly illustrated jacket, was listed as being hot from the pen of a best-selling author.

Her thoughts went round and round, like a squirrel searching for a hoard of nuts hidden and forgotten. It was a wearying form of mental exercise and it made her too exhausted to do anything but tumble into bed. Once there, she lay in the darkness, unable to sleep for the thought of Charles' careless mouth which had reduced her to a willing pulp and which had decimated her moral standards. She could still hear his voice in her mind—'Just a sample of the wares on offer'—and she could still feel the warm satisfaction of his arms about her. The best thing she could do with that feeling of warm satisfaction was to strangle it at birth! But it wouldn't be strangled, it wouldn't lie down and be dead! Not even when she went over all the things which should have killed it.

If Charles had a 'permanent' commitment, it was to his secretary, who called herself 'Mrs Smith', who was attractive without being strictly beautiful and who made no secret of the fact that she lived with him and had done so for five years that Roz knew of.

All the same, and at this point, she tried to cheer herself up; in a way, it was a feather in her cap to be propositioned by Charles Maine, if she wanted that kind of feather. Charles wasn't indiscriminate, he didn't spread himself around too much. Roz couldn't recall ever meeting any girl who had actually had an affair with him, but everybody seemed to know somebody else who had. Perhaps it was shop gossip, perhaps he hardly ever strayed from Mrs Smith, just the occasional little adventure. Mrs Smith seemed to be the permanent part of his life.

Which put her, Roz, in the category of an 'occasional stray adventure', a humiliating thought; nothing to be proud of, so she could take that feather out of her cap straight away. She groaned, heaved herself over in bed and thumped the pillow in a rage of self-disgust. She wasn't feeling in the least humiliated, she was feeling chilly and deprived so that if, by some miracle, Charles had opened her hotel room door and walked in, she would have welcomed him with open arms. It was a blessing that she was leaving London early the next morning.

Charles would ring her, she supposed, if the shots hadn't turned out satisfactorily, but she was almost sure they would be all right; he always said that he didn't like wasting film. She would go back to Sussex, spend a few more weeks with Eve, coping with the children and trying to get it through Stephen's thick head that she would never again be the worshipping acolyte, that the

time when she had prostrated herself before the
altar of his charm and beauty was long gone. The
effort involved would stiffen her moral fibre.

Stephen; her brain took that bone and worried
it in an effort to stop thinking about Charles.
What was it that Stephen wanted of her? She
didn't think it was an extra-marital relationship.
No, she had escaped from Stephen, she was no
longer on her knees before him; she was a de-
fector, and she didn't think he could stand the
thought of that. He was looking on her as some
sort of lost, strayed sheep and he was going
through the motions of trying to bring her back
to the fold because her defection had upset his
great big golden ego!

Her night of thought, which achieved exactly
nothing, caused her to sleep late, so that by the
time she had showered, dressed and breakfasted,
any hope of catching the early train back to
Brighton was out of the question, and as it was
Sunday, that was the only train which would get her
there in time to catch the one Sunday bus which ran
anywhere near Blackboys. She was further delayed
by a call to the telephone in the foyer.

Charles' voice came over the wire, cool and
rather amused. 'The pictures are O.K., I thought
you'd like to know.'

'Thanks,' she was terse. 'But you needn't have
bothered. I think I'd have preferred it if you'd
waited and got in touch with my editor. After all,
she's the most interested party.'

'My, we are in a bad temper this morning,
aren't we, darling?' Charles didn't sound in the
least put out and she thought that he must have

some psychic qualities. 'Didn't you sleep well?'

'I slept perfectly, thank you.' Roz could imagine him, lounging at ease, smiling in his mocking way, and she grew exasperated with him, with herself, with everything. 'And I wish you wouldn't call me darling,' she heard herself spit into the mouthpiece.

'Why not?' he was even more amused. 'It's a general form of greeting nowadays, there's nothing unpleasant about it and it's perfectly safe.'

Bitterness swamped her so that she abandoned her normally good manners. 'Oh yes, and I suppose that where you're concerned, it's not only safe, it's damn convenient. It saves you having to remember who you went to bed with!' And she slammed the phone back on the hook, aware that the young male receptionist was giving her a most peculiar look.

The little exchange didn't help her temper or her sense of ill-usage, but once aboard the train, she simmered down and gave her mind to the practical problem of getting from Brighton out to Blackboys. As far as she could see, she had three alternatives.

She could book into a Brighton hotel and wait until Monday morning; she could get a hire car to take her the ten or twelve miles or she could ring her home and have Stephen come and fetch her. The first two choices would be ruinously expensive considering that she hadn't earned a penny for the last three months, but even so, either of them was infinitely preferable to having Stephen collect her. That way wouldn't cost her a penny, but it could cost her goodwill.

At present, matters between her and her brother-in-law were on a strictly sister and brother-in-law footing; she had purposely kept it that way by avoiding any really close contact. But a half hour's journey in the confines of a car was another thing. Stephen would take advantage of it, he'd start on his 'togetherness' and his 'Wasn't it wonderful in the old days' themes. She would become exasperated with him and lose her temper, at which he would become kind and understanding until she screamed with frustration and possibly said all the things which she'd been bottling up since she had come back home, and they would finish the journey snarling at each other like a couple of Kilkenny cats.

Finally she decided on the taxi option. It would give her time, when she arrived in Brighton, to go on a hunt for the one chemist's shop which would be open on Sunday and she would buy Eve a very large bottle of perfume. She hoped the gift would boost her sister's morale and help her to get over the disappointment of never having more than three children.

Roz paid off the taxi and ran straight up to her sister's bedroom, only to halt inside the door with dismay. Sitting on a chair drawn up to the bedside, and looking as though sick visiting was part of his usual scene, was Charles. He was bandbox-neat and smart in a beautifully cut sports jacket and cord slacks which toned with it precisely; he was smiling at her in a very mocking way, and she glared back belligerently. This was an unwarrantable intrusion in her private life and she didn't like it. Her sister gave a glad cry of welcome.

'Roz, isn't this splendid? Isn't it a lovely surprise for you?' Eve was crowing with delight as though she had done something very splendid all by herself, as though she had personally magicked Charles out of thin air just for Roz's benefit. 'We've been waiting ages for you, but Charles is such good company, the time's flown.'

Roz manufactured a smile out of good manners, there was no mirth in it. 'Hello, darling,' she pointedly excluded Charles from the greeting. 'Have you missed me?' While she was asking, she handed over the extravagantly large flask of Arpège perfume which was the best which she'd been able to buy on a Sunday in Brighton. 'That's for being a good girl.' Her glance slid to the cot. 'Has the baby been fed?'

Mmm,' Eve smiled widely, 'and guess who gave him his bottle?'

'Don't tell me,' Roz kept the smile going, although it was so artificial, she thought her face would crack. 'Charles!'

'And he's found a name for him, isn't that nice? You know how I've been trying to get just the right name,' Eve had transferred her attention to the sleeping baby so that Roz felt free to scowl. 'Jasper,' Eve said it lovingly. 'Jasper Stephen. What do you think of that?'

'A bit highfalutin',' Roz wrinkled her nose. 'I go for the "Tom, Dick or Harry" thing myself, something simple, but I daresay I'll grow to like Jasper in time. Wasn't that always the name of

the wicked squire in those old Victorian melo-
dramas?'

'Mmm,' Eve giggled girlishly. 'We'll have to
hope that he keeps his fuzz of black hair, it would
be awful if he lost it all and went blond on us.'

'And you can, later on, get him to grow a
handlebar moustache to go with it. Then he'll
really look the part—a proper villain.' Over the
top of Eve's head, Roz stared stonily at Charles
and gave a definite emphasis to the last three
words. 'Where are the girls and Stephen?'

'The girls have gone to a birthday party at the
vicarage, Stephen dropped them off on his way to
Brighton.' Eve made a little face of distress. 'The
poor man had to go and see that ghastly post-
graduate student, she's having trouble with her
American studies. So I don't know when he'll be
back. Will you be able to fetch the girls, Roz?
About half past five, I think, so that the vicar and
his wife have time to get ready for evening service.'

'Mmm, anything else?' Roz rooted in her bag
for the neglected paperbacks and handed them
over.

'The cars,' Eve frowned. 'I've persuaded
Charles to stay for a few days, you'd better show
him where to put his car, and I've given him that
single room next to yours, it's all aired, but if
you'll make up the bed . . .' She sighed. 'What a
pity it will be if Stephen's late.'

'Not a pity,' Roz contradicted, 'a blessing. Start
praying that he doesn't arrive until we've put
Charles' car out of danger, he's quite likely to
drive straight through it if he's in his absent-

minded professor mood. Come along, Charles,'
she was brisk with a diamond-hard glitter in her
eyes. 'We'll put your car away first, we can collect
the girls in Eve's Mini.'

CHAPTER THREE

'ON second thoughts,' Roz paused in the corridor to allow Charles to catch her up, 'we'll see to your bed first,' and she collected sheets and pillowcases from the linen cupboard, maintaining an impersonal attitude which masked displeasure, but the masking wasn't strong enough so that the displeasure broke through before she was aware of it. 'You're spying on me, Charles. I thought you were above that.'

'Not at all,' he was urbane. 'I'm not spying, but neither am I above it if it suits my purpose. Actually, this visit is partly business, and I also have copies of your photographs in the boot of my car; I thought you might like to see them.'

'Scraggy and haunted?' Her good humour was returning and she could smile at him normally.

'No, just a little bit out of focus; deliberately so, of course, so that you look as charming as ever.' He accepted the pile of bed linen without a murmur and followed her.

'Speaking of charm,' Roz led the way down the corridor to the room where he would be sleeping and paused with her hand on the door knob, 'how did you know where to find me, and how did you get round Eye so that she was willing to put you up for the night?'

'The first was easy,' he waved aside any idea of

difficulty, while he grinned at her amiably. 'After you left my place on Saturday, I rang your editor at her home address. She told me where I could find you.'

'Just like that?' Roz raised her eyebrows until they nearly vanished into her hairline.

'Just like that,' he agreed complacently. 'You've been underestimating my powers, sweetie. A mixture of my charm and guile is well known to be irresistible; I don't usually use the mixture for that very reason, but I wanted to find you.'

'Business? That's what you implied.'

'Mmm. Yours and mine, but mostly yours,' he murmured, and there was the ghost of a laugh at the back of the words. 'There was this girl growing thin and pale; it was obvious to me that she was being starved of something . . .'

'In here, Charles,' she interrupted, flinging open the door on to a small, spartan room which was obviously unused. She took the pile of linen from him and dumped it on the bed. 'As you see,' she waved a hand round the room and her voice dripped honey, 'we don't go in for much in the way of sybaritic luxury. I hope it won't be too much of a contrast with your colour co-ordinated satin sleeping wear. But you ought to be able to ignore the clash for one night.'

'One night? Oh, no, Roz darling. Even I couldn't seduce you in one night, and certainly not on this narrow little bed. You weren't listening anyway—your sister has invited me to stay for as long as I like. Somehow she has the idea that you and I are at the beginning of something big and beautiful and she's ready to do her utmost to bring it to its passionate and inevitable conclusion.'

'Shut up!' she hissed at him rudely, her temper on the boil. 'One more word and I'll—I'll hit you!'

'No, you won't, darling.' His arm was about her and tightening painfully while his other hand encircled her throat. Had she been able, Roz would have put up her hands to cover her ears and shut out the sound of his voice which was no longer gently satirical, now it held a definite threat.

'Because, if you hit me,' his gaze was concentrated on the top of the stairs which he could see through the open door and he dropped his voice to a sibilant whisper, 'if you hit me, I'll hit you back, I'm no gentleman in that respect! I'll do it where it won't show but it *will* hurt.' And then his gaze came back to her face and his eyes lit up with a demoniac gleam in their dark depths. 'Smile nicely, Roz, and don't squeal when I kiss you. There's a very disapproving gentleman watching us from the top of the stairs. He looks as though he's going to blow a gasket! Is he the one you've been starving for?'

Her attempt to turn and look over her shoulder was stopped almost before it started; the finger around her throat slid up to her chin, holding her head tilted so that she couldn't move. Within a brief moment, she no longer wanted to; Charles' mouth teased her lips apart and she softened against him. Tears of humiliation welled into her eyes, tears for her own stupid weakness, and

Charles raised his head, reached for his handkerchief and wiped them away.

'Just another free sample,' he whispered mockingly in her ear. 'Do you like the line?'

Roz recovered herself swiftly and stepped back from him as far as the arm about her waist would allow her to go. 'No, I don't,' she muttered angrily. 'It's a bit brash and I don't think the colour suits me.' She half turned in the circle of his arm, aware all the time that it showed no sign of slackening. 'Hello, Stephen,' she caricatured a smile at her brother-in-law. 'Eve was getting worried about you. She thought you'd be stuck for the rest of the day with your post-grad student and Hiawatha!' There was a slight pause before she continued; it helped to steady her voice. 'This is Charles Maine, my photographer; Charles, my brother-in-law, Professor Stephen Berry. Eve has invited Charles to stay for a few days,' she added as though it was an extenuating circumstance.

'Charles Maine,' Stephen extended a hand, smiling with his best brand of bonhomie. 'Did they ever call you Charlemagne?'

'One or two did try.' Charles leaned back against the doorpost, pulling Roz back with him and holding her firmly so that she couldn't wriggle free, 'but they soon gave up.'

Stephen gave his great big glorious laugh and then became plaintive. 'I can't get my car in the garage,' he complained gently.

Roz seized on this with a breath of relief, glad that the conversation had taken a turn she could handle. 'We were just going to see about that when I'd made this bed up for Charles. If you'll

slip down to the village, Stephen and collect the
girls from the vicarage party, Charles and I will
have it all arranged by the time you get back. Better
call in on Eve while you're here,' she added as he
nodded and turned away.

'So that's your trouble.' Charles smoothed out
his side of the sheet and tucked it in, making neat
hospital corners. 'Your brother-in-law is suffering
from night starvation and he's making passes at
you.'

Roz raised a red face which could have been
caused by the effort of stuffing pillows into pillowcases. 'You do have a nasty mind!'

'Not a bit,' he shook out the top sheet and
tucked his end in. 'Not nasty, just practical. Your
sister told me she'd been an invalid for almost
three months and your brother-in-law looks the
virile type.' His mouth took on a tight, straight
line.

'You disapprove?' She raised an eyebrow.

'Everybody has their hang-ups.' He faced her
across the bed. 'Some men don't approve of
married women, I have this thing about single
girls and married men.'

'Sorry to disappoint you, but you've got it all
wrong,' She finished the bedmaking at top speed.
'But then you would have, wouldn't you? You come
down here, walk into a strange house among strang-
ers and start making snap judgments based on only
a few hours' acquaintance. You're almost bound to
misread the situation. There,' she looked at the bed
and around the room to see that he had everything
he would require, 'that's finished, now shall we go
down and sort out the garaging problem?'

Roz had difficulty in starting Eve's Mini, and for two pins she would have clouted it with something heavy, but finally the little car started with a sulky growl and she backed it out of the garage, the gears screaming viciously. She narrowly missed one wing of Charles' car as she swirled the Mini round in a tight circle and pulled it to a jerking halt on the grass verge of the driveway. She switched off the ignition and climbed out, shaking unaccountably.

'If that's the way you treat a car,' came Charles' hateful voice in a mild reproof, 'I shan't let you drive mine.'

Roz took one look at the enormous bronze-coloured Cadillac, eyeing it with reverential dislike. 'I wouldn't even try,' she retorted. 'I'd rather take my chance with a double-decker bus! Put it in yourself, where the Mini was, the other side of the garage is Stephen's.' And she swished off into the house, leaving him to dock his mini-battleship, collect his bag and follow her.

He caught her up on the stairs. 'Something tells me that I'm an unwelcome visitor, darling,' he murmured.

'How did you guess?' Her lip lifted in a delicate snarl. 'And don't call me darling. You know what I think of that.'

'If it's what you said on the phone, you couldn't be more wrong. It's the height of ingratitude to forget which girl you went to bed with, and if it was you, Roz, it would be an unforgettable experience.'

'And one which won't ever come your way!' It was with a definite feeling of satisfaction that she

let herself into the master bedroom, to find Eve
up and dressed.

'I'm coming down to see to dinner,' her sister
was determined. 'I've had enough of this lying
around like a dying swan—and don't make a face!
The doctors said I could get up for a while each
day.'

Despite Roz's forebodings, dinner was a pleasant meal. Eve provided Stephen with his healthy
salad, but she had made sure that other tastes were
catered for, so that while Stephen filled up on
lean meat and lettuce, there were thick steaks,
buttered new potatoes, asparagus tips and celery
with a cheese sauce for those who had less consideration for their health and welfare. Charles
was a good conversationalist and Stephen exerted
every ounce of his not inconsiderable charm, so
that when Roz and Eve left them to go and make
coffee, they were both quite amicably discussing
modern literature.

'He's a dish!' Eve eyed her sister conspiratorially. 'You're a dark horse, Roz, hiding
Charles under a bushel like that.'

'A typical case of mixed metaphors,' Roz
grinned. 'But you always did—mix them, I mean.
Actually, he's been very good to me as far as my
job goes. He's a marvellous photographer and
there are one or two shots where he's made me
look too good to be true. But don't get any wrong
ideas about him,' she warned. 'Once he gets his
hands on a camera, all the good humour vanishes
like snow in summer. He can be a dictator. The
first time I went to him, he told me to wash my
face and then he pulled the rest of me to bits

systematically. He made me feel like Hans Andersen's Ugly Duckling!'

'You never were ugly,' protested Eve. 'I remember you well, you were a lovely little thing.'

'And there speaks my sister!' Roz chuckled, and the conversation degenerated into childhood reminiscences until bedtime.

The next morning started well. Roz was up early to get breakfast for Stephen and little Freda; they would both leave the house at the same time and Stephen would first of all drive to the village to drop his elder daughter at the school before going on to Brighton and breakfast for them was a simple matter. Wheatflakes followed by a boiled egg, toast with a low cholesterol spread and homemade marmalade, all washed down with orange juice. Healthy, non-fattening food with not a poisonous chemical in sight!

It was also a silent meal, Stephen eating stolidly with such a smile of deep satisfaction on his face that Roz found herself wondering what he'd been up to. Then she took herself to task for having a nasty, suspicious mind; Stephen was merely pleased that at last Eve was showing signs of recovery. Freda was silent because she was reciting her multiplication tables under her breath. When they had gone, Roz made a fresh pot of coffee and took a cup up to her sister.

Eve was awake and out of bed, struggling into a cotton housedress and slippers, and at Roz's look of displeasure, she asserted herself. 'I'm coming downstairs and I'm going to start getting back into the swing of things. I feel miles better already just thinking about it. I was getting depressed staying up here in bed, out of touch, useless and worrying all the time. Don't scold, love; honestly, I won't overdo it, but it's a lovely day and I'm going to put Jasper in the garden in his pram.'

'But you'll have a rest this afternoon?' Roz was willing to give in, but not all at once.

'Promise!' Eve smiled widely. 'Carry your nephew downstairs, please, I'd never forgive myself if I dropped him.' She cocked an ear at a familiar sound. 'Is that Gilly yelling? Don't bother, I'll see to her.'

And although Roz had qualms about her sister doing too much too soon, she breathed a sigh of relief. Eve was definitely better, she was taking up the reins of management again. It might only be a week or so before she, Roz, could get back to London, to find herself a small flat or a commodious bedsitter and start thinking in earnest about her new career. No more worries about Stephen or Charles, they would be out of her orbit.

But at lunchtime the day went sour on her. Charles wished to take her into Brighton, he wanted to take some photographs of the Pavilion, and she was to provide the human interest. Of course, Eve agreed with every word he said—she would! Eve's eyes held a matchmaking gleam and while Roz longed to wipe that gleam away, which she could have done easily by explaining that Charles had nothing more permanent in mind than perhaps a tatty weekend or even a one-night stand, she lacked the courage to be so blunt. Eve liked Charles, it would be cruel to show him to her in his real colours.

Hence, she was on her way to Brighton clad in a yellow sundress with a small matching jacket and seated in splendour in the Cadillac. She hoped that he wouldn't be able to find anywhere large enough to park it!

Charles leaned across, taking one hand off the wheel to touch her bare shoulder. 'You don't freckle, I hope . . .'

'No,' she shook her head. 'I've a tough, thick skin, much darker than Eve's, and if I'm anywhere really hot, I go the colour of old leather. By Christmas, I've faded to a muddy beige which isn't very attractive, but it's not warm enough in England to do more than make me a shade darker than normal.'

Much to her chagrin, Charles found a parking ground close to the Pavilion, and a space in it large enough to take the Cadillac, and after making all the right adjustments, he spent nearly an hour photographing her against the forest of domes. She obligingly slipped from one pose into another, precariously leaning on weak-looking balustrades and going up steps and down them again at his direction.

'Isn't that enough?' she asked at last. 'What do you want all this for anyway? I've finished. Roz Wilshire has now joined the journalistic trade.'

'They're not for publication, not as advertisements.' He was serious. 'I'm entering the field of photographic art; you might even end up in an exhibition, if you're good enough.' He slipped the camera back into its case. 'Tea now, I think,' leading her with unerring accuracy to the best restaurant in Brighton. 'You probably need it.

'I was right, wasn't I?' He watched her as she poured their tea, in the tastefully decorated Chinese room of the restaurant which looked as though somebody had done it out to resemble some of the less hideous parts of the Pavilion. 'I said it was either a diet or a man, though I didn't allow for it being both, Oh, yes,' as she opened her mouth to deny it, 'your sister was most informative on the subject of her husband's health food craze. She knew you'd been sharing the rabbit food. My arrival gave her the excuse she'd been waiting for to get downstairs and start feeding you properly.'

Roz simmered under the surface. 'It's a very healthy diet,' she muttered, 'all full of roughage and so on. One gets used to it very quickly.'

'Not me, darling.' Charles looked at her sternly. 'There's a chance it may be served up to us all next time, and I'm not taking the chance. I saw a nice little place on the way here, and that's where we're going to have dinner tonight and every other night of my stay, if we can manage it. That way I'll be spared not only the healthy food but the languishing looks your brother-in-law keeps giving you.'

Roz, who had been filling the teapot from the hot water jug, set the metal container down with a distinct thump. 'That's a lie!' Anger drove the colour from her cheeks. 'Look here, Charles; I didn't ask you to come down here, I as good as told you that I didn't want your interference. I'm quite capable of arranging my own life, I'm a big girl now.'

'And still as stupid and starry-eyed as when you were nineteen!' At her look of surprise, he smiled nastily. 'Your sister loves you very much, she talks about you all the time. I've had your life story from when you were in rompers. Do you want me to give you a short résumé? The earnest young student who brought home her big, beautiful tutor to be admired and who had him whipped from under her nose by her sister? And then there was Stephen himself. After dinner last night, he became very loquacious, he told me the same story almost word for word.'

'If you don't shut up,' Roz warned, 'I'll throw the teapot at you. You've no right to draw conclusions or to sit in judgment. It's none of your affair. Go back to London and leave me alone!'

He leaned back in his chair and looked at her through a haze of cigarette smoke. 'I'm making it my affair. I told you I have this thing about married men and single girls, and besides that, I happen to like your sister. I don't happen to like the idea of her husband two-timing her.' A raised hand stilled her protest. 'Besides, if you recall, I've some goods on offer. I've already given you a couple of samples and as far as I'm concerned, you're my prospective customer.'

'And I should feel complimented?' Roz looked at him sardonically. 'I might if the goods were in mint condition, but I'm afraid I don't buy in the "used property" market.'

Charles raised his eyebrows at her across the table. 'You liked the samples, you can't deny that, and I don't think you've any reason to quarrel with the condition of the goods. People who live in glass houses . . . you know. And if I'm willing to overlook . . .' He broke off to watch Roz as she carefully put down her cup, collected her bag and jacket.

She was just rising to her feet when his hand came down hard on her wrist. 'Nobody walks out on me, Roz. Sit down!'

Roz perforce sat; it was better than making a scene, and there was a little voice inside her which warned that Charles wasn't afraid of scenes. He was probably a past master himself at making them and making capital out of them. Neither did she make a scene when, later, he pulled into the car park of a small country club. He switched off the ignition and consulted his watch.

'Just right, time for a drink before we order dinner.'

Roz made no attempt to leave the car, she sat stonily in her seat and looked at him through the window. 'I want to go straight home,' she said icily.

'Not a hope!' Charles grinned, not much and not kindly.

'You don't seem to understand,' her nose elevated at least three inches. 'I'm not dressed for dinner out, and besides, Eve will be expecting us back. It would be the height of bad manners to go off somewhere without letting her know.'

Slowly his eyes left her to wander up the length of a telegraph pole. 'We can let her know,' he murmured. 'This is Sussex, not darkest Africa. One telephone call is all it takes. Now are you going to walk in or do I have to carry you?'

Roz had been going to say, 'You dare!' but a

glance at his face was sufficient to convince her
that he dared! And with a haughty sniff, she slid
out of the car and slammed the door behind her
with sufficient force to set the vehicle rocking on
its excellent suspension. She made her telephone
call to an Eve who was quite phlegmatic and
unworried and then stalked into the ladies' room
to do a few running repairs.

The repairs took slightly longer than she had
expected but not as long as she had hoped. Her
usually smooth chignon was the worse for wear
and had to be completely redone, she had eaten
all her lipstick and temper had robbed her face of
any colour. Grimly, she applied herself to con-
triving a cool, sedate countenance and stepped
back from the mirror ten minutes later feeling
quite satisfied. But it was only ten minutes, and
she had hoped for half an hour! There was no
other way out of the ladies' room except the door
by which she had entered, so she sauntered out,
giving the impression of a young lady who was
looking forward to a cool drink and a good dinner
with no outward signs of the turmoil which was
raging within her.

Charles was waiting for her and a waiter
escorted them to a table in a secluded alcove although the dining room was barely half full.

'Martini?' Charles raised an eyebrow. 'We
could have gone into the bar to drink it, but it
seemed a waste of time.'

'With a lot of lemonade,' she stipulated, 'and
not too much of the fruit salad stuff on top.'

'You object to fruit salad?' The eyebrow went
even higher.

'I've been put off,' Roz explained. 'I came here once and had a Pimms No 1, and there was so much stuff on the top, I expected a knife and fork.' Good, she complimented herself, that's the way to do it; set the conversation at an ordinary level and keep it there. Charles would soon take the hint that she wasn't in the mood for anything deep or searching.

Charles didn't take the hint; he waited until the drinks arrived and then plunged into the deep end. 'How torrid was it, the affair between you and your brother-in-law?'

Roz removed the cocktail stick balanced across the top of her glass, which skewered a cherry between two slices of lemon. 'The temperature was normal for the time of year,' she said flatly, hoping he would abandon the subject, but she was disappointed.

'Your sister seemed to think it was nothing deep,' he murmured. 'She told me she would never have encouraged him if she'd thought it was anything more than a passing phase.'

Roz nodded serenely. 'Eve's generally right.'

'Then why . . .?'

'Leave it, Charles,' she shook her head at him. 'It was all a long time ago and I can't see why you should be interested.' She picked up the menu and became involved in a choice. 'I wonder which will be better, steak or beef Wellington? Steak, I think, they can't disguise that, and I'll have it with mushrooms.' This time he did take the hint, so that by the time they had arrived at the sweet course, she had almost forgotten how bad-tempered she was. The cream of asparagus soup was rich and soothing, the steak was thick and satisfying and the wine Charles had chosen was red and very dry.

Charles wasn't being objectionable; he sat quietly, paying little attention to his food, almost watching her eat, and just for the moment she was moderately happy with her world. She speared the last piece of her steak and then stopped with it halfway to her mouth. Stephen had just entered, and with a youngish girl, a blonde whose wide eyes were aglow with admiration and adoration. Roz had seen that glow in other eyes; she suspected that, seven years ago, her own might have looked just the same, and she gave an inward groan.

She glanced at her watch, nearly nine o'clock and then she looked back at Stephen and his companion who were being escorted to a table near the centre of the room. Charles followed her gaze.

'Jealous?' he queried, but she ignored him, reaching instead for her handbag and gloves, only to be stopped by his hand on her wrist. 'Sit down and finish your dinner.'

'No,' it burst from her in a savage whisper, 'I won't!'

'Yes, you will, Roz.' His tone was almost as savage as hers had been, but it lacked the smouldering violence. 'It's time you got over your youthful infatuation, and this is the first step towards it.'

'No,' she said again. 'Oh hell, Charles! You've got it all wrong, you don't understand . . .' How could she explain that it wasn't jealousy, not as he would understand it? It was the thought of Eve, at home and waiting, a table laid, a meal prepared. She tried to put it into words. 'Eve will be expecting him, she'll have dinner ready. It will probably be all spoiled by now and . . .'

'And you're not there to hold her hand?' His dark eyes surveyed her without any compassion. 'Don't be a fool, he'll probably have phoned her to say he'll be late. If you go home now with that look of doom on your face . . .'

'I want to go home.' She was stubborn about it.

Any other escort would have been suitably concerned, but not Charles, he was unmoved. 'Go, then! You've two options, you can walk or get a taxi, because I'm not taking you. Whichever you do, you won't arrive there a moment sooner than if you stay here and drive back with me.'

Her eyes sparkled with wrath, but she was spared saying any of the hot words which were bubbling in her throat by the arrival of the waiter with two portions of apple pie and a jug of cream. She would have liked to call Charles a pig and a bastard and any other unpleasant name she could lay her tongue to, but she was forced to smile sweetly and be silent. The dishes were set on the table, the waiter fussed about the condition of her dessert spoon and thoughtfully changed it for another one from a store of spare cutlery so that by the time she had started on her sweet, she had simmered down. Charles's next words sent her back to boiling point.

'Marry me, Roz. I'm willing to overlook your girlish indiscretions.'

The waiter was still hovering, so she turned her

face into a mask of non-expression and spoke with hardly a movement of her lips.

'How patronising can you get? What are you, some institution for the rehabilitation of fallen women? You overlook!'

'All right, I won't overlook it, I'll consider it as a mistake, and forgive you for being a little fool.' His lips twitched and there was a spark of humour in his eyes. 'Everybody makes mistakes and the wise ones learn from them. I'll credit you with above average intelligence.'

'Magnanimous!' Roz choked on her anger, while deep inside her a reluctant amusement stirred. 'And am I to overlook your past as well? Your secretary-cum-mistress who's lived with you for five years? You've the cheek of the devil, you remind me of . . .'

'. . . a guttersnipe?' he interrupted. 'But that's what I am! Are you going to be snobbish about it?'

Colour suffused her face. 'I'm not a snob! And I wasn't going to say "guttersnipe" either. I was going to liken you to one of those sweet, fast-talking market traders; like the barrow boys in Petticoat Lane, give them just a second and they'll talk you into buying anything.'

'Does that mean that given the chance, I could talk you into marrying me?' Charles looked relieved. 'Because I like your response, and you *have* responded. No, don't start denying it, you'd be telling lies. And I've the idea that if the relationship was regularised, it would be a response worth having. Underneath that cool, charming exterior there's a passionate wench hiding, and if marriage is what it takes to set her free, you've got it.'

Roz stirred her coffee and recklessly accepted his offer of brandy.

'Unusual!' He raised an eyebrow slightly. 'I've never known you to drink more than a couple of glasses of wine.'

'Dutch courage,' she informed him cheerfully as the brandy slid warmly down into her stomach.

'No need, Roz. When I have you, we're both going to be stone cold sober, and it won't be on the back seat of a car. And speaking of cars,' his hand silenced her protest, 'I think we could go now. Your brother-in-law is fascinating, or should I say overwhelming his little friend with his god-like aura, they haven't seen us so far, and if we go quietly they'll never know we were here.'

When Charles pulled the car off the road and under the shadow of some trees, Roz was not disturbed. Charles had said not in the back seat of the car and she believed him, but there was his remark about her response, and she wanted to be quite sure about it herself, she wasn't going to take his word for it. Responses altered with one's mood, and just at present her mood wasn't a very good one. Her temper had disappeared and she found herself filled with an aching regret—for what, she didn't know. She would let Charles kiss her and analyse her own response, but the moment he went beyond the bounds . . .

Ten minutes later she pulled away from him, bitterly aware that not once in that time had she thought about his secretary, not once. Which just showed the depths to which she had sunk!

'Leave me alone, Charles,' she spoke through the painful knot of tears in her throat. 'You've made your point, but it doesn't alter anything much. You've a low opinion of me and mine of myself isn't much higher. Leave me a little self-esteem, please; I don't think I can live without it.'

The house was in darkness when they arrived and Roz peeped into the master bedroom on the way to her own. Eve was sitting up in bed, reading a book by the dim light of the bedside lamp.

'You'll try your eyes doing that.' Roz was severe.

'So?' Eve smiled at her in the dim light. 'It's a good book and I want to finish it; my eyes will recover. Are you going to bed now, because if you are and you hear a noise later on, it'll be Stephen coming in late. He rang earlier to say he was still stuck with his post-grad girl and it was going to take a long time. Had a nice day?'

'Lovely!' Roz infused her tone with a spurious warmth. 'You'll have to come with us next time, Charles is very good company. Goodnight, love,' and she closed the door quietly behind her before making her way along the corridor to her own room.

CHAPTER FOUR

AFTER a night which seemed to have consisted of tossing and turning in between periods of deep and muddled thought, Roz, in a three-year-old cotton dress, came downstairs and made her way to the kitchen, arriving there a little later than usual. She had done her face after a fashion, a little tinted foundation and a cursory smear of lipstick; her hair was well brushed but tied back with a piece of ribbon which had seen better days and the dress, because of its age, was slightly faded and rather limp from frequent washings. Roz didn't care, she was not out to impress!

As she came to the bottom of the stairs the postman rattled the knocker and she crossed the hall to retrieve the bundle of letters which had plopped on the doormat. Riffling through the envelopes with busy fingers, she selected the one addressed to herself and pushed it into the pocket of her dress, then carried the remainder into the well equipped but old-fashioned kitchen where, for once, everybody seemed to have gathered.

Stephen was, as usual eating abstractedly while he read the paper; Eve, downstairs early for the first time, was spooning cereal into Gilly's ever-open mouth; little Freda was stoically wading through something which went snap, crackle and pop while reciting the alphabet backwards and Charles was sipping a cup of coffee.

As Roz entered, Charles looked up and gave her a quiet glance before he rose to draw out a chair for her.

'Sleep well?' he queried in a low murmur which only she could hear.

'Like a baby!' she answered, and hoped that her make-up was sufficient to disguise the faint violet shadows underneath her eyes.

Stephen grunted a greeting and Eve passed her a cup of coffee in between shovelling spoonfuls into Gilly's mouth, and Roz dropped the pile of mail on the table. She was waiting for a few minutes alone with her sister and the intervening period was going to pass with excruciating slowness, she could tell by the way in which Stephen abandoned his paper and sorted through the letters to select the big fat one with the United States stamp and then to toss the remainder across to Eve.

Freda spilled milk down her blouse front and had to be wiped clean; Gilly demanded more cereal, more milk, more toast, more juice until Roz was convinced the child would burst and then, when the kitchen was relatively free of breakfasters, Charles having gone for a walk in the garden, Eve started preparing the baby's bottles, loading the dishwasher and the washing machine while she tut-tutted over the amount of milky food which had been dropped or spat out on to the floor tiles.

'Oh, leave it, Eve.' Roz was feeling rather ragged, her nearly sleepless night had made her irritable. 'The daily will be here within a few minutes, she'll see to it. I want to talk to you.'

Eve nodded serenely. 'Come upstairs, then, it's

nearly time for Jasper's bottle. We can have a chat while he's guzzling it.'

Once in the bedroom, Roz flopped down on to a bedside rug and drew her knees up to her chin while she watched Eve collect all the paraphernalia which Jasper needed and install herself in a low chair with the baby on her lap. For a little while she did things to his rear end, ignoring his wails of protest, and then she offered the bottle to his other end and the cries died away into silence. He sucked on it fiercely as though he was dying of starvation and Eve crooned to him softly.

'I've had an offer,' Roz said baldly. 'An offer of marriage.'

If she expected cries of joy or surprise from her sister, she was doomed to disappointment. Eve looked up, still crooning.

'Why tell me? You've never told me before, and you must have had other offers; or are the men in London too choosy for words?'

'In London,' Roz grinned, 'there's a lot of competition.'

'So?' Eve raised her eyebrows. 'I still ask, why tell me? It's Charles, I suppose.'

'Mmm,' Roz frowned. 'What should I do, Eve?'

'Why ask me?' Eve grinned back at her. 'You've never asked me before. Sorry to sound repetitious, but you haven't, have you?'

'No-o.' It was a reluctant admission. 'But I didn't need to, not then. Those times, I knew it was "No".'

'And this time you're not so sure?'

'Something like that,' Roz admitted ruefully.

'On the other two occasions, I'd already made up my mind before the question was asked, so I knew what to say; but this time it's more difficult. The question came as a bit of a surprise and I'm not at all sure if I have a mind to make up!'

'Then in that state of mind or non-mind, you ought to say "No" or "Wait a bit".' Eve was judicious. 'Have you given it any thought?'

'All night!' Roz pleated the hem of her dress between thin, nervous fingers. 'I arrived at precisely nowhere!'

'Then how can I help, you silly girl?' Eve returned her attention to Jasper, who was going red in the face. She removed the bottle from his mouth and put him up over her shoulder to rub his back, he made a rude noise and his mother chuckled. 'Coarse little thing, isn't he? But never mind, he'll grow out of it. Roz,' she shook her head, 'I can't tell you what to do, I'm not in your shoes, and with the best will in the world . . .'

'. . . you're no use at all,' Roz grimaced dreadfully. 'I come to you for advice and help and I get nothing!'

'It's your life.' Eve became very serious. 'There's plenty of people who would be only too glad to offer advice, but I'm not one of them. You have to make your own mistakes, that way you'll have only yourself to blame if something goes wrong. I can only tell you one thing, and that is—when you get to the stage when you're willing to give him anything he wants, with no strings attached, then you'd better get married, because I don't think you're one of the modern types who could bear to be a live-in girl-friend. You're a bit of a puritan and also, you have a tidy mind.'

Roz went out of the bedroom in a little huff; then, as the door closed behind her, she had second thoughts and pushed it open again to put her head around the jamb and say sternly, 'You keep this to yourself, sister mine, or I'll pull your hair and drown your baby. No telling Stephen, not even a little murmur in the confines of your marital couch!'

Eve raised her head and across the room her eyes twinkled at her sister. 'That sounds much better,' she gave a youthful giggle. 'You're ashamed of yourself, and that's always a good sign—or do I mean a bad one? Hey! Don't go off empty-handed, take these nappies with you.'

Roz cleared away the clutter and then went along to her own room where she seated herself at the little desk in the window embrasure and read her letter.

It was from her editor, it was brief and concise and very flattering. Apparently, the magazine intended to give her a spread the month before her articles began. Roz was to be a real person and not just a face; she was to be shown at home, in the bosom of her family, therefore more photographs would be required, homey-type things. Roz Wilshire at her desk, answering reader's letters: Roz arranging flowers; Roz reading a book; Roz playing with the younger members of her family. At this point, her brows drew together in a bad-tempered scowl. And Mr Charles Maine knew all about it! He would make all the arrangements with her to take the required photographs! Roz went in search of him to scold.

'Why didn't you tell me?' she demanded crossly. 'Roz Wilshire at home!' She snorted down her small, straight nose. 'This isn't my home, it's my sister's, and it's quite possible that either she or Stephen will object to having their privacy invaded.'

Charles looked at her with dark, enigmatic eyes. 'Your brother-in-law object to a little publicity?' He made it sound like the eighth wonder of the world. 'I thought he thrived on it! You can tell him that *he* won't be in the pictures, if that makes any difference. They'll be you, with perhaps your sister in the background, all very cosy and conforming to the very best standards of domestic felicity.'

'Stephen will have to be consulted,' she grunted with displeasure. 'He could very well object . . .'

'. . . especially since he won't be in the photographs . . .'

'. . . And it could cause a bit of bother.' She glared at him.

'Then count me out,' Charles smiled bitterly. 'Family quarrels were never my forte.'

'Oh!' Roz looked and sounded surprised. 'Didn't your family ever quarrel?'

'No family.' He was curt and his face was now shuttered and withdrawn.

'You were an only child?' Interest stirred within her as she imagined him playing his solitary games; a small, thin, dark little boy, lonely and dreadfully alone.

He shrugged. 'I don't know. I grew up in an orphanage—and don't ask me if my parents were dead, because I don't know that either.' Perhaps he would have continued, but at that moment the front door slammed and Stephen strode into the kitchen. Roz smothered a swear-word—damn Stephen! He could always be counted on to put in an appearance just when he wasn't wanted and when it would be least appreciated. She had just begun to start knowing about Charles; he had started to open the door and now—she looked at his face—he had clammed up again!

Stephen exuded bonhomie. 'Can you spare me some time this morning, Roz? I've a free day and I've brought the notes for my lecture tour. I'd like you to go over them for me.' He turned to Charles, who was looking enigmatic again. 'You'll be able to amuse yourself this morning, won't you, old man?'

'Hardly,' Charles was not going to be co-operative. 'I need some extra equipment which means a trip up to London and I need Roz with me. Sorry, old man!' His mimicry was bitterly accurate. 'Are you ready, Roz? Because if not, you'd better step lively, we haven't a lot of time.' His hand was about her arm, pushing her in the direction of the door. 'Some other time, old man!' he threw the words over his shoulder.

'Very high-handed, if I may say so.' Roz, in a thin black suit with a primrose yellow blouse, installed herself in the front seat of the Cadillac and sat contemplating her shoes; high-heeled black patent pumps which made her legs look longer and her feet more slender. 'Rushing me off like that! I was just going to talk Stephen into a good mood.'

'His moods don't concern me.' Charles slid behind the wheel and switched on the ignition. 'We can manage very well without his permission.

I thought the house belonged to you and your sister.' He spared her a glance as he negotiated the curve of the drive. 'Eve told me that you were both born there and that she'd never lived anywhere else.'

'True,' Roz nodded. 'But I don't like the house very much. I suppose it's because I've been away from it for so many years. When I came back to it, I looked at it with new eyes. It's one of those pretentious, mock Gothic, Edwardian things and situated as it is on the outskirts of a village which looks as though it's been there for ever, it sticks out like a sore thumb. All that red brick! Perhaps, if it was suddenly transported to St John's Wood or Hampstead, it would be tolerable, but it's out of place in Sussex. Eve likes it though and I told her, years ago that she was welcome to my share.'

'It's a good place to bring up a family.' Charles was thoughtful.

'And that lets me out,' Roz smiled sweetly at him. 'Eve can bring up her family in it, but me, I don't have this maternal instinct.'

Charles nodded, his eyes never leaving the road. 'I'm glad to hear it. I'd like to establish a good relationship with my wife before we go into the Happy Families act. I want to know all there is to know about you and I'd like you to get to know me properly; it would take time and we'd do it more easily if there were no children to cope with while we were learning. There'll be plenty of time to start a family later, so would you object to four or five years without the patter of tiny feet?'

'If and when I marry——' Roz was being deliberately awkward and she knew it, but to her way of thinking, Charles was taking too much for granted. She pursed her mouth as though she was giving the matter a great deal of heavy thought. 'I think I'd prefer to start a family straight away. There's the matter of my age; I'm twenty-five, going on twenty-six, and I don't think I could afford to wait until I'm past thirty. Mothers should be reasonably young, I think.' She slid him a sideways glance to see how he was taking it and was disappointed to see that he was quite unmoved. 'Anyway,' she continued with relish, 'I'm sure that's a thing which concerns only my husband and myself, so there's no need for you to worry your head about it.'

'But I'm going to be that husband, you can make up your mind to it!'

'My, my,' she jeered at him. 'Until yesterday, the thought of anything as permanent as marriage had never entered your mind, and now it's bedded in firmly. It takes two to make that sort of bargain, perhaps you'd better remember that!' And she sank back in her seat with her eyes closed and remained uncommunicative for the rest of the journey. In the silence, she thought of a great many other things which she would say as soon as the opportunity arose and made a mental note of them in case she forgot.

It was nearly lunch time when Charles pulled up outside his house, and Roz found herself being surprised that it looked no different from when she had seen it last. The white paint still gleamed, the knocker shone in the sunshine and the two hanging baskets of flowers, one on either side of the door, had not wilted with neglect. Then she remembered that it was only—how long?—four days since she had been here last. It seemed more like an age!

'See to some lunch,' Charles directed as he pushed her in through the door. 'You'll find everything necessary in the kitchen.' And he headed for the stairs which led up to the studio.

There was no sign of the secretary, so Roz supposed the woman was also on holiday, and as she raked chops out of the freezer and delved among the neat packages of vegetables, she tried to recall what that secretary had looked like. It wasn't easy. Since the first morning five years ago, when she had come here for the first time, she had never really looked at the woman. After that, it had been just a wave of the hand as she passed through the lobby on the way up to the studio. She carried in her mind a memory of a woman, older than herself; always smartly dressed in businesslike clothes; blonde; well groomed, and that was all! The face—Roz smiled ruefully to herself; after that first time, she had never looked at it, and that first time she had been far too nervous for the face to make any impression. Margery Smith, she remembered that!

Of course, if she *did* marry Charles, the secretary would have to go! She, Roz, wasn't sharing! But the possibility was so remote that it could be discounted. Charles might turn her on, but he was a long way from her ideal when it came to choosing a husband, and what was more, turn on or not, she wasn't in love with him.

She remembered, with some embarrassment, her first love, Stephen, and how it had been then.

'A sickness of the mind', that's what the poet had said, but it hadn't been just her mind, not unless the mind controlled the body. She remembered the sick feeling in her stomach when she didn't have any lectures with him for two days, the hot embarrassment when he spoke to her and her tonguetied answers; they had come stumbling off her tongue, unreasoned because his sea blue eyes were looking at her.

No, it wasn't like that with Charles! Charles got under her skin and irritated her. For instance, here he was doing a King Cophetua act; *he* would marry *her*! He would be doing her a favour, that was what he made it sound like! Well, he could take his favours and donate them to some other worthy cause, she didn't need them. And she slammed the chops into the baking dish with some considerable force.

From the studio came the sounds of Charles; and he sounded as though he was turning out cupboards. There was the chink of metal, the pad-pad of his footsteps going back and forth across the floor, the opening and shutting of cupboard doors and drawers. Then he was on the stairs and Roz came out of the kitchen to see what was going on.

Already he had accumulated quite a pile of stuff in the small hallway; there was the big leather case which contained within its sponge rubber and velvet interior his treasured Hasselblad together with its extra lenses and filters. As she watched, he deposited a big tripod and a pile of chromium plated tubes which, when assembled, would make the frame on which he supported the spot lights.

'Oh, very professional,' she called as he turned to remount the stairs. 'It's always a marvel to me that other photographers can manage with a hand-held, 35-millimetre, single-lens reflex.'

At the top of the stairs, he turned to look down at her. 'But they don't make you look as beautiful as I do, darling, and they use ten times as much film. Stand still a moment.' He came down three steps and looked down at her intently. 'Yes, that's a good angle for your face, a bit foreshortened from this height, but you can get away with it.'

Roz went back to the kitchen and took out her bad humour on the plastic wrappings which shrouded the frozen peas and chips; tearing at them with angry fingers and letting the lid of the waste bin fall with a clatter after she had disposed of the rubbish. Charles came down the stairs again, and this time it must be his last trip with his last load, because he dumped more chinking stuff in the hall and came into the kitchen.

'Lunch ready?' he enquired, and came to stand beside her to check her preparations. Roz yawned in his face.

'Such as it is,' she murmured, taking the chops out of the microwave oven and putting them under the grill to brown off. 'You can set the table any time you like.'

When they had eaten and were sitting in the lounge, drinking coffee, Charles leaned back in his chair and surveyed her where she had tucked herself up comfortably on the divan. 'The meal was competent, but it lacked artistry,' he observed. 'Your sister neglected your education in domestic matters—a clear case of developing brain power at the expense of visual pleasure. Or don't you care how things look; except your own personal appearance, of course?'

Roz flushed but retained her cool. Eve had *not* neglected her education as far as kitchen chores went. If she put her mind to it, she could turn out a well planned, well balanced lunch or dinner with all the trimmings; a meal which looked as good as it tasted, although she made no pretensions to any particular ability. Today, she had been so bad-tempered that she hadn't bothered except to dunk a knob of butter on the peas.

She did her best to ignore the remark, to be silent while she drank her coffee and brooded on the injustices of life, but once again Charles had got under her skin to irritate her, to increase her feeling that she was being got at.

'I've been looking after my sister and her family for three months,' she told him icily, although the irritation showed through the ice, making her voice tart. 'Did you notice any signs of neglect or malnutrition?'

'A labour of love?' He smiled sarcastically over the rim of his coffee mug. 'Do I take it that today's little effort was only labour, that there was no love involved?'

Roz banged her own mug down on the tray, remembering her own first love and being upset by the thought of it. 'Love! What's that? And what has it to do with you and me? It's an emotion you don't know a thing about and it's one I don't trust. I've seen this so-called love in operation; I went through it myself when I was nineteen and I've seen other girls I know going through it—it's a kind of trauma. It flares up and then it dies and there's nothing left, not even the ashes of a memory to mourn over.'

'Your sister knows about it . . .'

'. . . That's what I mean,' she interrupted savagely. 'But we'll leave Eve out of it, if you please. She's perfectly happy because she's either as blind as a bat or she's trained herself not to see things, and I'm going to see that she stays that way. Well,' she slid off the divan and straightened her skirt, 'shall we go now? I'd like to be back in time for dinner.'

'Can't I tempt you to another sample?' Charles's smile glimmered across the room. 'I have several, I assure you, and each one is guaranteed to raise your blood pressure.'

'No, thank you.' She turned her attention to her appearance and picked a thread from the lapel of her jacket with finicky care. 'I've tried all the samples I need; I've assessed the quality of the goods on offer and I find them a trifle shoddy.'

'But not as shoddy as the line your brother-in-law is offering, surely?'

Roz sighed with exasperation. 'That has nothing to do with you,' she informed him, smiling a too sweet smile. 'So it would be better if you minded your own business. Shall we go?'

'As you wish,' he became compliant. 'You do the washing up while I load the stuff into the car,' and without waiting for a yea or nay he put his mug on the tray and went out.

An unreasonable disappointment filled her so that she carried the tray into the kitchen, ran hot water into the sink, squirted liquid in generously, even lavishly, and practically threw the dishes in after it. Having got her own way, she suddenly discovered that it was the last thing she wanted. She hadn't expected such an easy victory, she had actually been anticipating a fight, had been looking forward to it. Charles had asked her to marry him; no, that wasn't quite correct, he had *told* her that she was going to marry him. Not that there was much difference, the proposal had been made, and now he had offered a little lovemaking. She had refused and he had accepted the refusal without a murmur. He shouldn't have accepted her refusal so calmly, he should have shown some signs of fight, he should have . . .

Irritably, she scrubbed at obstinate sticky stuff on the plates and felt deprived! He was a mouse, not a man! He was an uninterested mouse!

'We'll find a place for dinner on the way back,' Charles was competently steering the car through the London traffic. He drove in the same way that he took photographs; economically, carefully and without fuss, the big car responding to his every touch. Roz looked at his hands, resting on the wheel, and had a sudden wild desire to touch them, to reach out and cover one of them with her own, but it was only a fleeting desire and easily overcome.

'I'm not dressed for dining out,' she pointed out reasonably. She was being difficult again and she almost wept for it. Why couldn't she have said 'that would be a lovely idea', or 'I know just the place'? She tried out the words in her mind and dismissed them, they made her sound weak-willed. So, to change the subject, to get on to something safer, 'Whatever made you buy a car this size?' Her hand waved round the huge interior and indicated the length of the bonnet.

'I like it.' He slanted her an amused glance as though he knew what she was thinking. 'The suspension is superb and it's very easy to drive, especially on long journeys.'

'But it must drink petrol,' she protested. 'Surely something a little less overpowering would have been more sensible.'

'What's "sensible"? I happen to like it, it's comfortable and distinctive . . .'

'. . . And ostentatious . . .' she interrupted.

'And ostentatious,' he agreed with her. 'Where shall we eat? That place where we went before, or can you recommend another restaurant? You know the area, I don't.'

'I told you . . .'

'Yes, I know you did, but I don't take easily to telling, and in any case, I told your sister before we left this morning that we wouldn't be back for dinner, so she won't be expecting us.'

Roz felt relief and a measure of pleasurable anticipation. He'd discarded his mouselike attitude! 'There's a good place just outside Lewes,' she made it sound grudging. 'It'll mean a bit of a detour, we'll have to go down to Lewes and back again. It'll mean an extra ten or fifteen miles, but I suppose . . .'

'You suppose rightly,' and the car sped on, not too quickly in the afternoon sunshine.

The country pub where they stopped for dinner wasn't very crowded, it was a pleasant place, so old that it was ageless, and it breathed a slumbering content from every brick and piece of timber. Tales were told about it—that it had once been the haunt of a gang of smugglers and that in the cellars there were still a few bottles of brandy which had never paid duty to King George the Third. Early on in life, Roz had believed the stories, that had been in her romantic days, but now she dismissed them. They were probably put about and fostered by the landlord for the sake of custom.

Roz and Charles were sitting on high stools at the bar, a solid sheet of shining mahogany; it was too early to eat and Charles had suggested a drink while they were waiting. Roz was just burying her nose in a tall glass of Martini and lemonade when she felt a hand clutching at her shoulder and heard a shrill, unmelodic voice in her ear.

'Roz—Roz Wilshire, isn't it? I'd know you anywhere!' and as Roz turned on her stool with a look of mystification on her face, the blonde young woman went on, 'You *do* remember me, don't you? Oh, please say you do, you can't have forgotten me!'

Roz delved in the depths of her memory and came up with a name. It wasn't the face she recalled, not the rather protuberant blue eyes nor the silky blonde hair, it was the voice. She remembered now, it was a voice which she had always hated; over-loud, piercing; a voice to jangle her nerves, and it had jangled them for a whole year. It had been the year of her finals, she was no longer in hall and this girl had shared the small flat with her.

'Vera,' she tried it out and it seemed to fit. 'Vera Lofts. I thought you went teaching somewhere up North.'

'Oh, I did.' Vera's giggle was just as bad as her voice, if not worse; it irritated Roz's already stretched nerves. 'But I've wangled my way back, and I'm taking my Master's. Won't you introduce me?' Vera's pale blue, probing gaze slid to Charles.

'Certainly.' Roz became enthusiastic. 'Vera, this is Charles Maine, my photographer; Charles—Vera Lofts. I roomed with her in my final year.'

Charles was not interested; his glance flicked over the girl, discovered several features that would render her unphotogenic and passed on to a leisurely and rather rude exploration of what was below her shoulder line. That apparently was unsatisfactory as well, so he returned his attention to his drink after a murmured, 'Hello'.

Roz hurried to cover what could turn into an embarrassing silence. 'What's it like at the U nowadays?'

'Still scandalous,' Vera giggled again. 'Remember that dishy lecturer, the one you had such a thing about?' Charles's scrutiny must have upset her, because she was putting the knife in, in earnest. 'He's married now, of course, but he's got this thing going with a post-grad student. Rumour has it that he's taking her with him to the States, a sort of consolation prize for doing his research notes for his lecture tour. Marriage hasn't altered him one little bit, all the youngsters still swoon over him and he still laps it up. I pity his wife.'

'I doubt she needs it.' Roz heard herself sounding disapproving, and then, out of the corner of her eye, she saw the flick of a white cloth. 'Sorry, we'll have to go, I think that's our waiter, trying to tell us our table's ready. Come on, Charles,' she made it sound hearty. 'I'm starving! Goodbye, Vera, nice to have seen you after all these years,' and picking up her drink she walked steadily into the dining room, hoping that Charles would take the hint and follow her.

'Bitch!' she muttered under her breath as she sat down at the table and then looking up to find Charles regarding her with an expressionless face. 'I think that little exchange has put me off eating.' Hastily she swallowed what was left in her glass and held it out to him. 'Can I have another, please?'

It set the tone for the rest of the evening. She drank her second Martini and lemonade swiftly, picked at her food and swallowed several glasses of wine thirstily to finish by asking for a brandy with her coffee.

'I know it's unusual,' she defended as she watched Charles raise an eyebrow, 'but I've this horrible taste in my mouth and nothing seems to wash it away. Maybe the brandy will burn it out.'

After the light and warmth of the pub dining room, the cool night air hit her like an icy blast. She wasn't drunk, she wasn't tipsy, she didn't chatter too much or giggle and she didn't trip over things. In the car, she mulled over Stephen's shortcomings. How dared he! How could he! Getting himself talked about, making Eve an object of sympathy, having her talked about and giggled over by a lot of chattering and gossiping students. She thought of what she would like to do to Stephen had she been big enough, and her hands crisped on her handbag so that her nails turned white under the colourless lacquer she used.

'You aren't big enough!' Charles seemed to pick up her thoughts. 'Stop getting so worked up about it. It's not you he's letting down, it's your sister, despite all the sweet nothings he murmurs in your ear when he thinks nobody's watching.'

Roz abandoned her slouched position and sat up very straight in her seat, staring out through the windscreen into the half dark. 'Bad manners, Charles,' she snapped. 'Stephen is my brother-in-law and I love my sister.'

'But I'm excused, aren't I?' He sounded bitter. 'My upbringing wasn't of the mannerly type, more dog eat dog and the last one alive's the winner. One thing I did learn, though, and that's not to kiss and tell. You should get Stephen to take lessons in that. He tends to dwell on his conquests.'

'You've been talking to Stephen?'

'Say rather that Stephen has been talking to me, only when you weren't there, of course.' Charles looked amused. 'No conversation complete without a eulogy on the excellence of Professor Stephen Berry. I've never known a man so much in love with himself!'

'But if he *is* taking that post-grad girl with him,' she harked back to what was foremost in her mind, 'what are we going to do?'

'We?' The dashboard light showed his surprise. 'I'm going to do nothing, and neither are you . . .'

'But I can't . . .'

'You can,' he was unsympathetic. 'And you will. Just nothing, it isn't your business!'

CHAPTER FIVE

THROUGH the open french window, Roz could see Eve and Charles seated together on the swing hammock. They were deep in conversation, and just for a moment she felt a twinge of envy. They had no right to get on so well together, they only did so because Eve didn't know the ins and outs of Charles. He was showing her his 'party' face, and it was unfair that he kept that face for Eve.

It would be ironic if, for the second time in her life, she lost her man to Eve, but that would be fate, because Eve was just as good-looking as she was and had a far nicer nature. She was warm and loving, sympathetic too, not the mass of prickles which was Roz Wilshire. With a little sigh, Roz buried herself again in the pack of photographs which depicted the latest fashions from Paris.

She was doing an exercise, trying to pick out the various trends and then tone them down for everyday wear, to give a forecast of what the big multiples would make of the extreme garments in the photographs. It wasn't a serious attempt, nobody was going to publish this bit of work, but she stuck at it grimly, making quick, deft sketches of wearable clothes; clothes with the same line but with the more extravagant excesses removed or toned down.

The originals took too much wearing, she decided. They might be all right on a youngster who wanted to make a splash, but she was trying to remember that the magazine readership embraced thousands of women from sixteen to sixty and very few of them were five foot eight tall and had figures like beanpoles. A slight noise behind her made her drop her pencil and turn round to see Stephen entering the sitting-room.

'All alone? That's nice,' he gave her a confidential smile. 'It's so rarely I have an opportunity to speak to you.'

'Any time, Stephen.' She gave an inward grimace; Stephen was going into his cloak and dagger routine and she wondered who he was going to stick the dagger in. Outwardly, she smiled, a pleasant, noncommittal smile which meant precisely nothing. 'It's not as though we had anything secret to discuss,' she continued. 'There's nothing Eve can't share, or Charles either, for that matter.'

'Oh, Charles!' Stephen's golden glory was slightly tarnished by the chill in his sea blue eyes. 'What on earth do you see in that fellow, Roz?'

She grinned to herself and wondered what Stephen's reaction would be if she said 'sex appeal'; he would probably think she was a little mad. 'It's working together so much,' she explained gravely. 'We have a common interest in that, and of course we both know the same people.'

'We worked together once.' He sounded rather regretful, as though the past was infinitely preferable to the present state of affairs.

'Mmm,' Roz smiled widely. 'A long time ago, though and I was dreadfully impressionable. The good old bad old days when I was growing up—a very painful process. Thank heaven it only happens once in a lifetime.'

'I hurt you when I married Eve?' He drew nearer.

Roz kept her smile going while she drew back in her chair. 'If you're hoping I'll say 'yes' you'll be disappointed,' she said tartly. 'At the time, I admit it felt like a deathblow, but now I know better. Calf love's like that, it's too intense to last. Looking back now, I find it all rather a bore.'

'Do you, Roz?' He moved nearer still and, huddled as she was into the back of the chair, she could retreat no further. Stephen clasped her shoulders firmly and lowered his head to an intimate lack of distance so that his eyes shone into hers; his were filled with a supreme self-confidence which set her teeth on edge. 'Weren't they the best times?' he murmured huskily as he sought her mouth with his own. Roz twisted slightly, but he was too quick for her and his lips claimed hers hotly.

'Naughty!' Charles' voice came from the open window where he and Eve were standing together, having walked up from their seat on the hammock. Stephen raised his head swiftly and Roz did an automatic survey. Eve's face registered worry and a hurt which tore at her heart, Charles' had a mocking expression, but Stephen's embarrassment, if he had any, which Roz doubted, was hidden by his beard.

Charles stepped through the window and gently

disengaged Roz from Stephen's grasp. There were white patches of temper at the sides of his nostrils, he gave her one contemptuous look, but as he stepped back, his face changed as though somebody had wiped off the contempt with a cloth. He came erect, registering nothing but a loving reproach, except for his eyes, which were hard and filled with a cold rage.

'I thought we'd decided to break the news at dinner tonight.' Even his voice was reproachful and he looked at Eve with a sad smile. 'We're engaged. Did your sister always spoil surprises?'

The hurt cleared from Eve's eyes, to be replaced with a matchmaking glow as she looked from Roz to Charles and back again. 'You mean. . . .' Oh, Roz, you little beast, you could have told me first!' She shared Charles' reproach, but it was a laughing, real emotion; not assumed as his was.

'I meant to,' Roz summoned up a cheeky grin, 'but Stephen was here and you weren't. I was dying to tell somebody, and when I saw you and Charles so cosily together in the garden, I thought *he* was telling you. Stephen's very pleased,' she added with a malicious look at her brother-in-law. 'He'd got the idea that I was heading for a desiccated spinsterhood, hadn't you, Stephen?'

Eve rewarded her with a beaming smile. 'You always were secretive—it just shows what love can do.' She turned back to Charles triumphantly. 'It's loosened her tongue. We'll have a party to celebrate . . . It's ages since we did any entertaining . . . I can't wait . . .' and she grabbed her husband's arm and towed him to the door. Roz

watched them go, Eve still enthusing and Stephen
looking as though he was glad to escape, and only
the door closing behind them cut off Eve's excitement.

As soon as they were alone, Roz whirled on
Charles, the words which she hadn't dared say
before coming in a forceful stream. 'What the hell
do you mean, misleading Eve like that? How dare
you! I haven't haven't . . . I wouldn't . . .!'

'. . . But this time you will.' Charles' fingers
closed on her arm and she squeaked with pain.
'You should be congratulating me on some quick
thinking, not snarling like an angry cat. Or would
you rather I'd left the explanations to you?'

'I wouldn't have told lies . . .'

'No?' He gave her a shake which made her teeth
rattle. 'Then enlighten me; how would you have
explained that touching scene to your sister?' His
voice changed to a mockery of her own high, clear
tones. 'It didn't mean anything, Eve . . .'

'And it didn't!' Roz was smarting under the
injustice of his implied accusation. 'It was just
Stephen up to his tricks. Eve would have under-
stood . . .'

'Then you weren't looking at her face,' he
interrupted. 'You haven't given any thought to
the situation here. Eve's not been able to be any
sort of wife for months, she's been expecting
Stephen to stray, she even mentioned that post-
grad student—making rather a sad little joke
about it. She's made herself accept that, telling
herself that out of sight's out of mind; but her
own sister! And in her own house, right under
her nose!'

'How dare you! I told you, you don't understand . . .'

'Oh yes, I do! Your sister's a wonderful person,
and for some reason she finds it hard to talk to
you,' the sneer in his voice came over clearly.
'She's been needing a sympathetic audience and
I've just been providing it, so you can take that
superior look off your face. She needed somebody
to talk to and I'm a stranger, unconnected. I
learned a lot, and when we came to the window
and caught sight of that touching little scene, I
was watching her face. The last thing she expected
to see was *you* leading her husband on, so I
covered for you. Now, you'll carry it through. I'm
a great believer in the sanctity of marriage.'

Roz opened her mouth to let out a vitriolic
stream and then shut it again while she exchanged
vitriol for vinegar.

'*You*! You believe in the sanctity of marriage!
That's a laugh!'

'Laugh this off!' Charles jerked so that she
came hard against him. His hands left her arms
and she found herself firmly held. One arm was
about her waist while his other hand was tangled
in her hair, holding her head still. She tried to
wriggle away, but the hand tightened and pulled
so that she thought her hair must be coming out
by the roots. 'Give,' he muttered fiercely as his
mouth came down on hers, hard and angry.

When he raised his head, Roz sobbed; her scalp
was smarting and her lips felt bruised. 'Animal!'
she whispered, trying to kick at his shins. His foot
came behind hers to hook her off balance and she
fell back in the chair with him on top of her. 'I

won't . . .' And then her protest was cut off as his mouth found hers again. Only this time it wasn't savage and angry, it was warm and seductive, compelling a response. The hot sweetness uncoiled within her and she found herself softening against her will. She sobbed with humiliation as her hands went up to his head, holding his mouth against hers, and everything dissolved in a blur of feeling and wanting so that when she felt his fingers on her breast, she moaned and arched against him.

It seemed an aeon of delight until Charles raised his head and looked down at her. The angry light was gone from his eyes and amusement curved his mouth. 'Bloody uncomfortable,' he murmured. 'Why couldn't you have collapsed on the couch? But you look suitably rumpled and flushed.' Without haste, he did up the buttons of her silk shirt blouse, his fingers lingering on her neck. 'I've bruised you a bit.' He didn't seem in the least sorry. 'Come on, Roz, let's go and see what treats your sister has in store for us.'

Roz pulled herself together and stepped past him to stand in front of a handy wall mirror. It was a convex one and her image was distorted, but it was good enough to ensure that she was tidy and neat. 'It's only a front,' she threw the words over her shoulder, 'just for Eve's benefit. I've no intention of letting it go any further than a sedate engagement which will last only as long as you're here—and if you start pawing me again, I'll slap your face in public!'

'You won't, Roz.' His arm went about her waist as they moved towards the door. 'I'd slap you

back and kiss you silly, in front of everybody; and
I could do that, I've just proved it.'

'Brute!' her fingers went to her swollen lip as if
she could still feel the pain of it. 'I don't like your
samples!'

His arm tightened about her waist and his
fingers closed, pressing hard on her rib cage.
'That wasn't a sample,' he reproved her. 'It was
part of the main stock, and you *did* like it. Try
being honest for a change.'

'And I won't have a ring.' Roz adjusted her safety-
belt, sat back in the car seat and looked mutin-
ously determined. 'It's no use you buying one,'
she added. 'I won't wear it.'

Eve had started this—Roz glowered at the
countryside. Eve had dripped a cloying sweetness of
engagement rings, love evermore; white weddings
and The Voice that Breathed o'er Eden. It had only
been cloying to Roz. Eve and Charles had seemed to
be enjoying themselves, Charles had aided and
abetted in Eve's worst excesses, he had even looked
faintly regretful when Eve had displayed her own
engagement ring.

'I don't wear it much,' she held out the large
diamond solitaire. 'To be quite truthful, I didn't
like it half as much as the one he wanted to give
me. That was an heirloom—his grandmother's, I
believe; rubies, but I knew I mustn't have it. I'm
always taking rings off, you see; washing up and
so on, and I'd have been sure to lose it. This at
least is replaceable.'

'Orphanage brats don't have heirlooms,'
Charles said quietly, and Roz raised her eyebrows.

So he'd told Eve that! But then of course he would; Eve would have winkled it out of him and been gently sympathetic, going overboard to show him that, as far as she was concerned, it made no difference. She would have been kind and sweet, saying something like: 'It doesn't matter that you never knew your family, we'll make it up to you. We'll be your family from now on.' She would have pointed out that now he had a readymade family, a sister, two nieces and a nephew, not to mention a brother, and Roz wondered how Charles had taken that!

'I understand that a ring is essential,' Charles gave her a mocking grin. 'It's what convinces everybody.'

'Oh, if that's all you want, something to give this farce an air of reality, I've plenty of junk jewellery and some of it looks very good, so you needn't bother,' she said ungraciously.

'Not good enough,' he shook his head. 'There's no mistaking the real thing, and I'd hate for somebody to start thinking that the engagement might be as phoney as the ring. We'll see what we can get in Brighton.'

'But it is a phoney,' Roz protested. 'Damn you, Charles; what are you up to? You *said* it was a cover-up to help Eve, and now you're acting as though it's all in earnest. You're letting a little bit of makebelieve go to your head!'

'Not in the least.' Charles didn't look at her, it wouldn't have been convenient; they were waiting at a quite busy T-junction. He studied the traffic and then slipped easily into the stream. '*You* were the one who grabbed at the cover-up, the results of a guilty conscience, I suppose. All I did was offer you a way out, you took it, and now, darling, you'll stick to it.'

'You mean you're taking all this seriously?' Her voice rose from its normally controlled tones to an outraged squeal.

'Certainly.' He sounded rather amused. 'It might be all a game to you, but I don't play that sort of game. When I play, I play for keeps.' The amusement was gone and he sounded grimly resolved. 'I've drafted out a notice for the papers, the usual thing: "A marriage has been arranged . . . and will take place . . ." and I shall send it in as soon as I've applied for the licence and made arrangements with the Registrar. It's high time you were wedded and bedded, you're lethal running around loose.'

'I will not choose one,' Roz raised her chin and her lips firmed. Her voice dropped to a hissed whisper. 'You can show me every damn ring in the shop and I won't pay any attention!'

'You don't have to choose,' Charles was unmoved. 'You'll have what you're given. Ah, that's better,' he nodded approval as the jeweller took away the tray of diamond solitaires and replaced it with one which showed a little more colour. 'This, I think.' Charles picked out an opal surrounded by a sparkling rim of diamonds. 'You're not superstitious, I hope, darling?'

Since the jeweller was regarding them closely, Roz smiled sweetly. 'I was born in the right month, *darling*,' her voice was syrupy. 'In any case, the only unlucky thing about opals is that they're rather soft, they damage easily; even immersion in water isn't good for them. In fact, the less they're worn, the better. I'll have the opal.'

Secretly, she admired the stone greatly, although nothing on earth would have made her admit it. The opal sat there against the black velvet background and through the veins in its opalescent milkiness, streaks of blue, green and red fire glittered balefully, making the sparkle of the diamonds seem commonplace. It was beautiful and she wanted it—but not as an engagement ring. Almost automatically, she started doing little sums in her head and came to the sad conclusion that she couldn't afford to buy it for herself. Her spell off work had reduced her bank balance to less than two hundred pounds, and this ring would cost far more than that.

Impassively, she watched the jeweller give the ring a final polish, put it in its little leather box and accept the cheque which Charles had written. Equally impassively, she watched Charles open the box, take out the ring and slip it on to her finger where it sparked turquoise and red fire dangerously. Dangerous—yes, that was the word. She would have to tread very carefully if she was to get out of this mess without a husband. Charles as a husband she couldn't accept, her pride wouldn't permit. She would need to trust the man she married; she didn't expect him to be as pure as driven snow, but a five-year-long liaison with his secretary was too big a pill to swallow. No doubt they had parted amicably, but ... She could accept a love affair or two, but one that lasted for five years? No, it would be like breaking up a marriage, and she would feel as though she was stealing. That was another thing which her pride wouldn't allow.

But, she decided, since Charles had never raised the question of his secretary, she could hardly do it. The best thing was to play along with him and take a chance of escape as soon as it arose. Roz walked along the pavement with him, going she knew not where; she hardly noticed the people passing and the shop windows were a blur. It wasn't until she stumbled over a high kerbstone that she raised her head and asked where they were going.

'Register office.' He was curt. 'The sooner we apply for a licence, the sooner we can be married.'

'How soon?'

'I believe three days' waiting is necessary.' The hand on her arm tightened as if she was going to run away, which she wasn't. Instead, her mouth curved in a smile of wolfish glee.

'The exercise will be useless,' she told him, hardly bothering to conceal her triumph. 'Quite useless—you're wasting your time.' His raised eyebrows tempted her into displaying malicious glee. 'You can't get a licence without certain information, and I'm not giving you any help in that direction.'

His smile, as he looked down at her, was as wolfish as her own, and he led her into the entrance of a small shopping arcade where he reached into his breast pocket with his free hand while controlling her with the other. When his fingers emerged from the tweed of his jacket they were holding a folded piece of paper, one dog-eared corner of which displayed some red lines.

'Your birth certificate.' His wolfish smile became a positive leer as he flicked the fold of paper open and waved it under her nose. 'Eve parted with it without a murmur. I told her it would be a great help if the original could be found; it would save us getting a copy.'

'You-you conniving bastard!' Outrage sparkled in Roz's eyes. 'And I suppose you have your own with you?'

'I never travel without it.' Charles was now serene. 'It was one thing which the orphanage was very definite about. We were always taught that we ought to have some method of identification about our persons. I also have my passport. Checkmate, darling?'

'Not in the least.' Now that the shock was over, she was beginning to enjoy herself. It was a battle of wits and she was sure that with a little concentration, she could win. 'I'll concede you one small pawn and we'll play out the rest of the game.'

She sat quietly in the Registrar's office while Charles arranged the licence, her smile was remote as she accepted the Registrar's congratulations and good wishes, and she didn't open her mouth until Charles and the Registrar had arrived on what, to them, was a suitable date and time for the small ceremony to take place.

'Impossible, darling.' She didn't shout it or even snap it out; instead she said it with a mournful shake of her head and a melting glance at the Registrar which begged him to make allowances for the stupidity of her husband-to-be. 'My sister,' she explained. 'She's arranging a lovely party for us, it would break her heart if anything happened to spoil it for her.' Concealed from the Registrar's gaze by the front of his desk which possessed a truly magnificent, polished mahogany modesty board, her high-heeled shoe ground down on one of Charles' pigskin casuals, and she wasn't kind about it; she gave her heel a definite twist before she raised her foot.

'One can't give an engagement party for a married couple,' she was almost pathetic. 'It's quite unthinkable!' The Registrar bent his head to his diary and out of the corner of her mouth and in a voice which only Charles could hear, she murmured, 'That one's mine! Your move, *darling*!'

Charles' smile was rather forced and Roz felt a despicable satisfaction. She could have broken his toes, she rather hoped she had, at least one anyway! 'When is the party?' he mouthed back at her, and she shrugged her slender shoulders.

'I haven't the faintest idea,' she whispered, 'but if I have anything to do with it, I should think it would take place next Christmas, which gives you six months to make the arrangements.'

'Bitch!' he whispered with a fond smile, and then aloud, 'We seem to have reached an impasse,' he absorbed the Registrar's nod with equanimity, 'and my fiancée did so want to be a June bride! But that leaves us three weeks, doesn't it; perhaps if I rang you within the next few days, when the arrangements are slightly less fluid . . .?'

They went for lunch in the same restaurant, and

the clientele seemed to be composed of the same well dressed, beautifully coiffeured ladies. Roz looked at them and wondered if that was their life; a little walk around the shops, morning coffee, another period of window shopping followed by lunch; then perhaps a bit of serious shopping, possibly in a cut price supermarket before they came back here for tea. A little smile curved her lips, nothing to do with the well dressed ladies but brought on by her small victory in the register office. She stared hard at the gold dragons which writhed across a black japanned screen which shielded the door to the ladies' powder room and concentrated hard.

It wouldn't be wise to be too euphoric just because she had thrown a spanner in Charles' works. It had only been a very tiny spanner and it would soon be mangled up. Then his machinery would go on running smoothly and she would be processed through it like a can of baked beans, or should it be like one of his photographs? Taken, developed, printed, washed, dried and glazed; all with care and attention to detail but with a ruthless efficiency. Roz tried to think of a few more spanners to throw in the works, but she was distracted by some delicious celery soup, the necessity of deciding between breaded veal and mushrooms and chicken espagnol, not to mention the array of various sweets.

Her appetite was healthy and unimpaired by the thought of the licence nestling in Charles' pocket; that was something she would think about later. Just for now, she was a hungry young woman who would think better on a full stomach. Charles took his cue from her and gave most of his attention to his food until they were at the coffee stage when, stirring his cup automatically, he observed.

'This should set your golden boy back on his heels!'

'Yes.' Roz's smile glittered with the quality of chipped ice. 'He'll now, possibly, turn his full attention on to his post-grad student, who looks as though she'll be a pushover. You shouldn't have interfered, you should have used your head. One moment's thought would have told you that I'm not such an easy proposition. That student will say "baa" and follow wherever he leads.'

'No,' there was a fugitive twinkle in his eyes, 'you're not much like a sacrificial lamb, are you, my sweet? You've got nasty pointy teeth.'

'And you look like a satyr,' she told him snappily. 'You've got nasty pointy ears—and don't think this lamb is going to spread herself on the altar without making a fight of it!'

'You fight very well,' he murmured. 'And I shall have the bruises to prove it. I thought you were going to break my toes.'

'Didn't I?' Her face registered regret. 'I'm so sorry. Ah well, better luck next time!'

She kept up the acid bickering all the way back in the car and felt much better for it, but when they arrived, it was to find Eve up to her ears in party arrangements, and Roz went back to feeling that she was being got at.

'You're going to knock yourself up, sister mine,' she remonstrated. 'You're not over the baby yet, you're not well enough.'

Eve pooh-poohed her. 'Of course I'm well

enough. It's just what I need, something to really wake me up, get me out of this baby-bound fog I'm living in. Not that I don't love the baby—I do, you know I do, but he has to take his place in the scheme of things. I've made out a guest list, it's quite small really; is there anybody you want to invite?' The question was addressed to both Roz and Charles, and as one person, they both said 'No'.

'Then,' continued Eve happily, 'there's just the vicar and his wife, the couple from the schoolmaster's house, those very nice people who took over the farm and run a riding school, and I thought we'd have a couple of dons and a tutor or so from the U. The dons will be practically moribund, but their wives are very nice, and of course, we shall have to have Stephen's post-grad student; that's why I'm inviting a tutor or so. The poor girl will want some young company.'

'That's eighteen people at least,' Roz protested. 'It's far too many, think of the food we'll have to cook!'

'Caterers,' Eve brushed aside the objections. 'And isn't it a good thing that this is such a big house, we can open up the doors between the sitting room and the drawing-room, take up the sitting-room carpet, borrow some records from the neighbours . . .' and in a haze of planning, she went off with her pad and pencil clutched tightly in her hand to count napkins and cutlery.

'Now see what you've done!' Roz scolded. 'My sister has the bit between her teeth. Thank God we're not in London, she'd probably have booked the Dorchester!'

Charles chuckled. 'Leave her alone, Roz; she's enjoying herself. She's looking better already. Why don't you do your part and find her something really splendid to wear?'

'But all this hoo-ha about a farce of an engagement!' Roz found herself near to tears.

'Eve doesn't think it's a farce and, for that matter, neither do I,' he sounded quite serious. 'Just think about it for a moment, will you. Would I have gone to the trouble of applying for a marriage licence if I hadn't been serious? Make up your mind to it, Roz; we're going to be married.'

'Not if I have anything to do with it,' she stormed, 'and you can't marry an unwilling bride.'

'Unwilling?' he gave a short laugh. 'Oh no, Roz. I'm sure I shall have your full co-operation.'

'Get *lost!*' she yelled at him as he went upstairs to his room to change.

Eve chose this moment to come back, but her mind was too occupied to be bothered by a small matter like Roz shouting rudely up the stairs. 'The glasses,' her brow creased in a frown. 'We've only a dozen of each, now what's to do? Shall we use what we have and hire some more or would it be better to hire everything? It would save us washing up and all that bother.'

'Hire it all,' Roz muttered fiercely. 'Hire the glasses, the cutlery, the crockery, half a dozen waiters and a butler, if you like. I don't care,' and she collapsed on the bottom stair while tears slowly welled up in her eyes and spilled over to run down her cheeks.

'Pre-wedding nerves,' Eve diagnosed without

any signs of being disturbed. 'I wept buckets myself, I know how it feels. You get this feeling that things are out of control.' She plumped down on the stair with Roz, taking her sister's hand, and then, just as Roz was thinking she'd get some much-needed sympathy, Eve spotted the ring. 'Oh, it's lovely,' she crooned. 'Charles has very good taste, hasn't he? Lots of men would . . .'

'Lots of men wouldn't rush me off my feet,' Roz wailed. '*Do* something, can't you? I want a long, long engagement. I don't want to be married for ages, I'm very happy as I am.'

Eve patted her hand. 'Silly girl, don't get so uptight; it'll be all right on the night.'

Roz found no comfort in this at all, in fact it sounded like the knell of doom, so she raced up the stairs and locked herself in her room. There, she flung herself on the bed and hammered the pillows with clenched fists. She was being forced, manoeuvred to do what she wanted to do. She wanted Charles, she loved him, despite the fact that he was the most hateful creature in creation, despite his thinking that she was . . . At this point, she ceased her hammering and angry mutterings, and pulled herself together, washed her face and redid it, brushed her hair into some sort of order and went back downstairs determined to be as awkward as possible while preserving a cool, calm and collected front.

CHAPTER SIX

Roz opened bleary eyes and gazed at the streamers of sunlight filtering through the curtains, then she rolled over in bed and closed her eyes again firmly. Yesterday had been the most awful day in her life—far worse, now she thought about it, than the day when Stephen and Eve had told her about their forthcoming marriage.

She looked down at the ring on her finger. It was now milkily bland with not a hint of hidden fire. Of course, that was a trick of the light, it wasn't an omen or anything silly like that, but a shiver ran all the way up her back and then down again. Was it only yesterday Charles had put it on her finger? It seemed like a hundred years ago; that was the worst thing about time, when you were happy, it whistled by, but a little bit of worry, of uncertainty, and it dragged on leaden feet.

Last evening had been ghastly because Stephen had talked to Charles. Well, he hadn't talked to him, he'd talked at him and she, Roz, had sat at the dinner table going hot and cold by turns. Stephen had been full of good humour and advice for the husband-to-be, and although Charles had been very non-committal, brushing it all aside, Stephen had gone on and on. The man, she thought viciously, had the hide of a rhinoceros and about the same amount of tact!

And he wasn't above implying things either. To listen to him, one would have thought that Roz's youthful infatuation had involved far more than it did. Of course, he didn't say anything which was utterly false, but he seemed to have the gift of colouring facts very slightly and forcing his audience to draw false conclusions. Or maybe it was just her imagination, a slightly guilty conscience perhaps at having made such a fool of herself all those years ago. Come to think of it, she was slightly ashamed of herself!

Unable to sit listening any longer, she had escaped to the kitchen with Eve. Yes, it had probably been all in her mind, because Eve hadn't noticed anything. She had thought that Charles and Stephen were getting on together famously! After the kitchen had been tidied and the table set for breakfast, Roz had gone off to her bedroom, locked herself in and had sat staring out over the garden until it was too dark to see anything any more. After that, she had slipped into bed, switched off the light and prepared herself for a wakeful night.

Some time around dawn, she had slipped into an exhausted sleep which had been peopled by a faceless Margery Smith and Stephen, who had both chanted that she must leave Charles alone, and when she had turned to him in bewildered terror, he had walked away from her, leaving her alone in the darkness.

With a disgusted grunt at her own stupidity, she slid out of bed, grabbed her robe about her, stuffed her feet into her slippers and padded off to the bathroom, where she found her sister

coping with a recalcitrant Gilly who didn't want
to be washed.

'You ought to have another bathroom put in,'
Roz growled. Lack of sleep and an overdose of
worry had made her bad-tempered. She caught
Gilly's soapy little body as it was trying to escape
the cleansing process and redeposited it in the
bath. 'You stay there this time, my girl, or Aunty
Roz will beat you!'

'All the best books say you shouldn't say things
like that,' Eve smiled widely. 'It's supposed to
make the kids nervous.'

'Nervous!' Roz snorted. 'Look at her, she's
about as nervous as a suet pudding!' She made a
horrid face at her niece, who demonstrated her
fright by shrieking with glee and slopping water
all over the floor while she implored her aunt to
'do it again'.

Finding a bath impossible at the moment, Roz
went back to her room where she flung open the
wardrobe doors and contemplated the contents.
Charles had said she should find something super
for Eve to wear at this ghastly travesty of a party
and she casually flicked through the hangers until
she came to a white tricel knit dress. Her nose
wrinkled at the chilly memories it evoked.

She had worn it for a travel ad. about Greece
and she recalled standing barefoot against a Doric
column made of polystyrene, in front of a backdrop which showed the Parthenon in vivid sunlight against a cloudless sky. She had been pour-
ing grapes and other fruits of the earth out of a
plastic cornucopia, the heating in the studio had
been on the blink and she had nearly frozen to

death while Charles, warmly wrapped in a duffel coat, had snarled at her to stop shivering.

Carefully she drew the dress out of its plastic cover and examined it. She had only worn it once and sent it to be cleaned straight away; it looked as good as new, so she would give it to Eve, not lend it, and as a bonus, she would take up the hem the required two inches.

By this time, she judged, the bathroom should be empty, and she pattered along the passage and after locking herself in, she stood under the shower, her mind busy with Eve's hairstyle, which would have to match the Greek lines of the dress; and the make-up, of course. The idea was to turn her sister into something resembling a Vestal Virgin, and with Eve's face, that shouldn't be too difficult.

Dressed and looking trim in a pleated, swinging skirt and a pink silk shirt, she met Eve at the top of the stairs and they went down together.

'You're a bit grumpy this morning,' Eve raised her eyebrows. 'Do you want to cry on my shoulder?'

'Cry!' Roz's voice raised an octave or two. 'Today's no day for crying. Today's the day for smiles all round. Charles is going to take blasted photographs.'

'Then, if you can't work up a better smile than that, you'd better say "cheese".'

'I feel more like gorgonzola, a bit blue and maggoty.' Roz sniffed and changed the subject. 'I looked in your wardrobe while you were at the invalid stage and it's time you put that floral chiffon in the dustbin. I've found a dress for you for the party, I've only worn it once and I'll make you a present of it.'

'But the chiffon's a nice dress.' Eve was protesting, but not much.

'It was a nice dress,' Roz sniffed again, this time disparagingly, 'Five or was it ten years ago! Time you had something new.'

'My, we are in a mood!' Eve chuckled. 'Come and have some breakfast before you bite. Stephen and Freda have already left, Gilly's playing outside, so we'll have the kitchen to ourselves.'

'Where's Charles?'

'In the kitchen, of course, making some fresh coffee. Oh, I see what you mean, but Charles is different . . .'

'He's different!' said Roz with a snap of her teeth, and glared at Eve's serene face. 'You know I don't really want to marry him, don't you?'

'You say it, but I don't believe it.' Eve was still serene.

'Well,' Roz halted on the staircase to put her head on one side and consider. 'I don't and I do, if you see what I mean.'

'Yes, I know what you mean,' Eve giggled, and went on down the stairs.

In the kitchen, Roz looked moodily out of the window on to the patio where Gilly was trying to beat a worm to death with a leaf. She ignored Charles who was fiddling with the coffee filter machine and turned back to her sister. 'That child has sadistic tendencies,' she remarked surlily. She was uncertain of herself and it was making her irritable. She accepted the cup of coffee which Charles offered in silence and then glittered at him. 'And you, maestro, how do you want me this morning; town or country elegance, or will you settle for sackcloth and ashes? Your wish is my command.'

Charles paid no heed to her bad humour; he looked at her thoughtfully and nodded. 'Very much as you are, neat and wholesome. That skirt will do nicely and so will the shirt, but loosen your hair a bit, it looks too severe. And we'll have a pair of flat shoes or sandals, please, those slippers have seen better days.'

'Blame that little monster.' Roz gestured to where Gilly had relinquished her efforts to murder the worm and was now stalking an insect. 'She sloshed water all over them. Heavens, Eve, go and stop her, do! She's caught something and I think she's going to eat it.'

When her sister had gone flying through the door, Roz swung back on Charles. 'I-do-not-want-to-marry-you!' she said slowly and distinctly. 'Well?' and she glared at him, the word a challenge which she emphasised by banging her empty coffee cup down on the table.

Charles poured her another cup of coffee, unmoved. 'Sit down, Roz, and stop raging. The matter is out of your hands, you've no choice. You behaved stupidly and without thought, I pulled you out of the mess you landed yourself in, and from now on you do as I say—and at present, I say "Curb that bad temper of yours".'

'Thank you so much!' She lifted her lip in a snarl. 'I'm like this every morning, hell to live with, you'd go mad in a week. Call it off and I'll tell Eve we've settled for a short affair. How's that?'

'It sounds disgusting.' He made his mouth prim so that she almost laughed at him. 'Marriage sounds so much better, more—er—respectable. Of course, I shall lay down certain rules and I shall expect you to abide by them.'

'A policy of non-interference on both sides, perhaps?' she suggested, and his reply shook her.

'You get one inch out of line, darling, and I'll interfere all right.' Eve was just outside the window, but he ignored that, they could have been alone on the moon or on a desert island. His hands were on her shoulders to jerk her against him. When he judged she was at a suitable distance, he released her shoulders to hold her firmly with one arm about her slender body and the fingers of his other hand grasping her chin firmly.

This time Roz started melting long before he kissed her. She watched his eyes close as his face came down to hers and was lost, her body softened to his touch and her arms went about his neck, her hands grasping his hair to hold him to her.

'Think you can stand it?' he whispered in her ear a little while later while she licked her swollen lip and tried to focus her bemused eyes.

'Oh,' she snapped back to normal and tossed her head, 'My powers of endurance are phenomenal. It comes partly of being a much photographed model and partly from being pure in heart. My strength is as the strength of ten—you know!'

'Which isn't quite the impression I gained from your randy brother-in-law.'

'Oh, Stephen,' she dismissed him with a wave

of her hand. 'I know you don't believe me, but
Stephen can't help it. He has this Narcissus com-
plex, he likes to study his reflection in female
eyes.' Her voice died away as her original plan for
tarting up Eve expanded and took definite root in
her mind. Stephen always hated competition, he
wasn't used to it, and it drove him mad. Suppose
he had a little competition, suppose she made Eve
the cynosure of all eyes so that Stephen melted
into the background; how would he react?
Knowing Stephen, she thought the results might
be dramatic!

'Charles——' she began as she attempted to free
herself of the arm about her waist, but he showed
no signs of slackening his grasp. 'Charles, listen
to me! I'm going to make Eve look stunning for
this party she's giving. Would you mind looking
at her with appreciation, deep appreciation,
please?'

'I already do,' he smiled down at her in a
devastating fashion. 'To put it bluntly, my
sweet, your sister is one of the most naturally
beautiful women I've ever seen. I could look at
her all day, in a purely appreciative way, of
course.'

'Then please do.' She was tart. 'Please concentrate all your aesthetic appreciation on my sister
and *leave me alone!*'

'Quite impossible!' He looked down at her, his
eyes mocking. 'She doesn't want me and you do.
I can't bear to see you unfulfilled. Besides, you
must remember we're engaged. I wouldn't dream
of looking at another woman, not in that way.' He
accompanied this with a short, hard and mirthless

laugh as he whisked her away to start the photography.

Roz managed to look kind, sympathetic and efficient in a variety of poses; in a chair, at her desk, in the garden with a pair of secateurs with which she was making a pretended assault on a rampaging creeper, and all with Eve doing something anonymous in the background. It wasn't as easy as working in the studio, the spotlights had to be moved bodily from place to place, but these were informal pictures and she didn't need to look at the camera, which helped enormously.

At last Charles pronounced himself satisfied so that she could relax, take the kind, sympathetic look off her face and let her thwarted soul show through while he took a couple of shots of Eve and the two younger children for the family album. For that, he didn't need an audience, in fact he told her quite brusquely to go away, and, left to herself, she mooched back to her room for another good think.

It was no longer a matter of Charles turning her on, it had gone way past that as far as she was concerned, and he seemed willing to have her even though he thought she and Stephen had . . . But could she be equally generous? That was the problem! Could she ignore Margery Smith and the hold she had on Charles? Somehow, Roz thought she wasn't that generous! Perhaps if it had been a relationship of shorter duration, she could have brushed it aside, but five years . . . In five years, people grew together.

No, she decided, she couldn't turn a blind eye to something which had lasted that long, it wouldn't be either wise or sensible, and anyway, her damned stupid, stubborn pride wouldn't let her. She would wake up in Charles' arms, in the middle of the night, and feel ashamed of herself.

The thought of Charles and herself together in a bed brought a hot flush to her face and set her trembling, so, with a hurried step, she went along to the bathroom, washed her hands thoroughly and came back to load a needle with white thread and start taking up the two-inch hem around the bottom of the Greek dress. She concentrated on what she was doing, making the stitches small, neat and hardly visible, so that after ten minutes or so she had calmed down.

Dinner was at half past six on the night of the party, and it was a very scrappy affair. Eve had spread the kitchen table with some bowls of salad, a plate of cold meats and a basket of rolls while, in the dining room, the caterers had set up trestle tables against one wall, covered them with white cloths and laid out what looked like a Scandinavian cold table in excelsis. Then they had all disappeared, after threatening to return at some unearthly hour the next morning to collect the crockery and glasses.

'You've had nothing to eat.' Charles caught Roz on the stairs as she was going up to do Eve's hair and face.

'I'm not hungry,' she answered blandly. 'I'll have something at suppertime, there's enough food laid out to feed a regiment.' But she continued up the stairs vaguely comforted by Charles' concern.

She allowed herself half an hour to turn Eve

into a cross between a Madonna and Helen of Troy and then went to her own room to achieve an Oriental look which she had decided would be a nice contrast to all that Greek purity. The look was based on a straight yellow silk dress, perfectly plain except for some heavy embroidery and the knee-high slit on one side of the slim skirt. To this she added a slicked-back and polished hairdo and held the heavy knot of hair at the back of her head with a couple of gilt-headed pins. When she stepped back from the mirror to get an overall picture, she felt satisfied. Despite this being her engagement party, she had been determined that Eve should shine brightest, and as far as she could see she had succeeded. Then pinning a bright, charming smile on her face, she went downstairs to greet the guests.

The first part of the evening was a dreary bore and uncomfortable. Roz winced inwardly whenever somebody wished her well or shook Charles' hand while they congratulated him on his good fortune, the vicar was fulsome, the post-grad student simpered and made no attempt to hide her adoration of Stephen, one of the dons had an ethnic wife who reproved Eve for having chairs. Everybody in their house, she said, sat on the floor as nature intended, it was so much better for the posture.

Charles caught Roz up at the buffet where she was loading her plate with smoked salmon and vol-au-vents filled with creamed crab.

'You're not looking at Eve enough,' she hissed at him from the corner of her mouth. 'You promised.'

'I was knocked over in the rush and trampled flat,' he excused himself, and gestured to where Eve was surrounded by two youngish tutors and her husband. 'She has a remote, untouchable air, don't you think? She looks as though she's operating on another plane.'

'Upstairs with the baby, I expect.' Roz was flattening. Eve was not ethereal or remote, she was earthy and warm and her thoughts were rarely away from her family.

'I've arranged the wedding,' Charles murmured in her ear as she made up her mind about shredded carrots in a vinaigrette sauce. 'This is the party which was the stumbling block and now it's nearly over. We'll be married on Wednesday!'

Roz managed a smile because several people were watching. 'It sounds like a life sentence,' and she turned her attention back to the laden buffet table where she decided against the carrots and chose asparagus tips instead. 'Wouldn't you rather set me up in style and have your own private latchkey?'

'Nothing so reprehensible.' His eyes slid over her thoughtfully. 'We're going to be married,' his tone was mockingly virtuous. 'It's so much more respectable.'

She choked on a piece of salmon; that Charles should be talking about respectability! When her eyes had stopped watering, she flicked him a glance from under lowered lids. 'I wasn't thinking of anything that far ahead. I had something more elastic in mind.'

'No,' he shook his head as he deliberated about the lobster patties. 'There won't be anything elastic about our relationship, my dear. It will conform strictly, with the accent on "strict".'

Roz concealed her temper adequately, contenting herself with an answering nod. 'And if I refuse? If I just go on eating my supper and tell you that as far as I'm concerned, the deal's off . . .'

'Unwise, darling, and it might be painful.'

'You'd beat me?' She raised a haughty eyebrow.

'With pleasure!' and he moved aside to make room for the ethnic lady who was deploring the absence of sunflower seeds and who heaped her plate with the despised carrots as a sort of consolation prize. When she had gone, Charles moved in again.

'Wednesday!' He was firm.

Roz shook her head and looked at him pityingly. 'No, I can't do that,' and before he could open his mouth to say something humiliating and hurtful, 'Eve,' she explained. 'She wouldn't understand the rush.'

'And I don't understand the delay. You took me up quickly enough when it was a matter of saving your face. Are you playing for time, darling?'

'The thing I most like about you is your trusting nature.' If Charles could be scathing, so could she.

'I'm noted for it,' she caught the derisory gleam in his eyes. 'In any case, my plan has your sister's full approval. Being so happily married herself, she naturally wants you to go and do likewise. She quite understands our desire to get married as soon as possible, I believe she's afraid our ungovernable passions will get the better of us.'

'Our passions!' Roz drank the contents of her wine glass—a very superior vintage which should have been treated with more respect—in one gulp.

'Mmm.' She suspected she was being made fun of and she didn't like it. 'Unlike you,' Charles continued smoothly, 'your sister thinks I'm devastating and devastatingly right for you. She thinks I'm a chance in a million and she quite agrees that you shouldn't let any grass grow under your feet.'

'I don't believe it, you're making it up! When did all this discussion take place?'

'When I was doing her photographs.' He looked at her cynically. 'Both you and Golden Boy underrate your sister. She may lack your academic qualifications, but she's no fool. She'll be a lot happier when you're safely married.'

'I'm glad you have somebody's happiness at heart,' Roz snapped out the words while maintaining an expression of sweet adoration for the benefit of the guests.

Charles collected her empty plate. 'I aim to please,' he murmured, 'like, I've made some fresh coffee, it's in the kitchen, would you like a cup? It's said to be good for irritability,' and he gripped her arm firmly and started to lead her out. Roz was glad, she was relishing the thought of a break from so many curious eyes. A break when she could let her hair down and say just a few of the biting, hurtful things, even yell them if she felt like it—but her hopes were doomed to disappointment. The ethnic lady cornered them before they could reach the safety of the doorway.

'And when is the wedding to be?' She was arch.

Roz jerked as if she had been caught in a volley of buckshot, but Charles rose to the occasion. He swung her round, laid a long finger on her lips and looked down at the lady with half humorous approval.

'I've been waiting for that question all evening,' and he said it in a tone which was perfectly audible throughout the dining room so that nearly everybody halted, forks halfway to their mouths and plates tipped dangerously. 'We're going to be married on Wednesday. It'll be a very quiet affair at half past twelve in the Register Office in Brighton, but we hope you'll all join us at the hotel afterwards.' And amid congratulations, he hauled Roz out of the room and into the kitchen.

'Why did you tell them that?' she wailed, feeling that she was being driven into a corner.

'It seemed appropriate.' He was non-committal. 'Don't look so stricken, Roz. I made the arrangements yesterday and you've had plenty of time to get used to the idea. Just think of it—from Wednesday on, you'll be able to concentrate on me exclusively, and you will, won't you, dear?' It sounded more like a threat than a promise of happiness everlasting, and she quailed. 'We'll go up to town tomorrow morning,' Charles added, 'and we'll be staying overnight so pack a few things.'

'Why?' She buried her nose in her coffee cup, refusing to look at him.

'Me, to work,' he was reasonable, 'and you, to get something to be married in.'

'But I can do my shopping in one morning,' she protested. 'We don't need to stay overnight.'

'I shan't seduce you.' In this present mood he was unreadable. 'You can have my bed—you ought to get used to sleeping in it. I shall make do with the divan in the lounge.'

'But . . .' she broke in, only to be silenced as he interrupted her interruption.

'I want to process those colour shots of you and you can make yourself useful in the kitchen. You're going to be the wife of a hardworking photographer, so you might as well start getting used to that as well. Now, come and dance, they've started the music.'

Roz could hear the stereo blasting out and became strangely shy. 'Won't they wonder where we've been?' she asked hesitantly.

Charles shrugged. 'Does it matter? They'll probably think we've been canoodling in the garden, so I'd better kiss you to make it look authentic.'

He was going to kiss her whether she liked it or not, so there wasn't much point in making a fuss. Besides, Roz found herself in need of some reassurance; Charles was making everything sound very coldblooded. There wasn't much reassurance about the kiss, it was far too demanding, but he made it perfectly plain that he wanted her and she found herself responding with far more enthusiasm than she had ever displayed before.

His hand slid down the curve of her spine, wandered around her hip and pulled her against him. She followed his lead shamelessly, but when he raised his head eventually to whisper, 'Starved,

aren't we?' she blushed hotly. She wanted to
giggle, but a giggle was more likely to end in
tears.

'Definitely rumpled!' He surveyed his handi-
work with satisfaction as he adjusted the neckline
of her dress. 'Fix your hair, my sweet, you look as
though you've been pulled though a hedge and
keep your chin up—the worst hasn't happened
yet, I'm reserving that for Wednesday night.'

'And making it sound like an execution!' She
raised her head and tried out a gay, uncaring
smile. 'How's that?'

He looked at her critically. 'It wouldn't fool
me,' he told her sardonically, 'but it'll give the
others the right impression.'

Roz glanced down at her ring where it sparkled
fierily through the milkiness. 'Does Eve know
we're going tomorrow?'

'Mmm, I told her earlier today while we were
having a chat.'

'You talk to her a lot,' she raised an eyebrow.
'You tell Eve earlier in the day, but for me you
wait till the last moment!'

'Jealous?'

'Yes, I am', she wanted to shout at him, but
she did no such thing. He was kind to Eve, he
talked to her, joked with her, but all Roz received
was an occasional hot look which started her
burning inside. She wanted tenderness and
caring, not the look which implied that all he
wanted was to get her into bed with as little delay
as possible.

The rest of the evening passed in a haze of
unhappiness and doubt which she covered with a

carefully charming smile, but once in bed, she added up the successes of the evening and found there was only one. Nobody had been worshipping Stephen! He'd had competition and from the quarter where he'd least expected it, from his own wife, and Eve had won hands down. The postgrad girl had offered him adoration, but he'd been so jealous of the attention paid to Eve that he'd shown the girl he didn't want her, not on her knees or even flat on her back! Roz sighed before she turned over to sleep. She was becoming very coarse, and that was all Charles' fault.

After a very early bath, Roz dressed herself elegantly for town and carefully folded a few things into an overnight case. This morning there was no limp, much-washed cotton dress or scuffed two-year-old sandals, neither was it the time for a flannel skirt, silk shirt and a pair of lace-up shoes. This morning was the thin, black suit with an old cameo pinned to the lapel, a creamy silk blouse with a hint of lace about the neck, fine tights, high heeled black patent pumps and her hair drawn smoothly back into a chignon.

When she had made her bed and straightened up the small clutter in the room, she tumbled the contents of a drawer to find the handbag which went with the shoes, pushed her cheque book into it with her purse and a hankie, picked up the overnight case and went out and along the passage. From below, she could hear voices; Eve's high and clear as she chatted gaily and the deeper tones of Charles as he answered, together with Gilly's yells of frustrated fury about something. She was nearly at the stairhead when a dressing-gowned

Stephen caught at her arm, halting her progress.

'Oh, good morning,' she said brightly. 'Sleep well?' It was only something to say, she couldn't have cared if he'd walked the house all night.

'Mmm.' Stephen's eyes slid to the overnight case. 'Off to town early? Where are you staying, at a hotel?'

'No.' He had stopped so Roz had to stop as well. She put down the case with a thump and straightened to face him. 'I'm staying at Charles' place.'

'I don't like the sound of that!'

'Oh,' her eyes twinkled, 'aren't you being a teeny bit old-fashioned, or are you having a morning after the night before? It was a lovely party.'

'Not bad,' Stephen said grudgingly.

'And Eve,' Roz enthused, her eyes sparkling wickedly. 'Didn't she look marvellous? The rest of us hardly got a look in.'

'And I didn't like that either.' His face was tight with displeasure. His gilded self-satisfaction was tarnished and wearing thin so that the small ugliness was showing through. 'The way she was practically flirting with those young fellows *and* Charles right under the noses of a couple of University wives! It could cause a lot of gossip.'

'Never mind,' she comforted him sweetly, honey dripping from her tongue, and then she lashed out with the sting. 'It'll only take the place of the other gossip, won't it? I mean the lot I heard about you and your post-grad girl. From what I can gather, everyone's laying bets as to whether she'll go with you on your American tour. Oh,' as she saw his face darken, 'don't blame me, I haven't been spying, nor did I have to dig for the information. It was handed to me on a plate over the bar of a local pub, if you must know, and it was in a loud voice and accompanied by the usual wink and nudge.' She allowed her contempt to show through. 'Really, Stephen, you should be ashamed of yourself! You're a married man, a father of three children, and that girl's nearly young enough to be your daughter.' At this point she became angry. 'And *you* have the nerve to object to my staying at Charles' place!'

'I don't care for the fellow, Roz.' Stephen was giving himself time to make a recovery. 'I don't think he's good enough for you. Apart from the tales he tells, we know nothing about him.'

'But you aren't marrying him,' she retorted. 'I am, on Wednesday.' And as she said it, she realised it was true. Come hell or high water, she was marrying Charles. Not because she'd been pushed into a corner and it was an easy way out for her but because it was what she wanted to do. The difficulties, his secretary and anything else she found, she'd worry about those when she had to. Somewhere along the line a lot of her pride had dropped away and all that was left was an overmastering desire to belong to Charles. Maybe it wouldn't make for an easy life, maybe it wouldn't be a particularly happy one, but it was the one she wanted.

'When are you coming back?' Stephen interrupted her euphoric thoughts.

'Tomorrow.' She was blithe now. 'Charles and I . . .'

'Don't bring him back here,' he interrupted. 'Leave him in London or put him up in a hotel.' His sea blue eyes glittered spitefully. 'I don't want him in my house!'

Roz's nostrils thinned with temper, she opened her mouth and let loose. '*Your* house, Stephen?' She lifted her chin and looked down her nose at him. 'But it's not your house, is it? It's Eve's and mine.' It was an unforgivable thing to say, but she didn't care. It was time somebody told him a few home truths. 'Charles is here at Eve's invitation and I don't object. So he stays until Wednesday—and,' once started, she thought she might as well go on and let him have the rest of the broadside, 'I hope I don't have to listen to any more scandal about you and that student, so I'll give you a piece of advice. If you want somebody with you on this American tour, take Eve. She'll wow them, or is that what you're afraid of?'

'Eve can't come,' he protested. 'The children . . .'

'. . . will love it, all except Jasper, and he won't mind where he is as long as the bottles and clean nappies keep coming. Yes, I think that's a very good idea,' she stilled his objections with a wave of her hand. 'You take your family, dear brother-in-law, or I might be tempted to start a little scandal myself, always making sure that it got to where it could do the most damage.' She looked him straight in the eye. 'Now I've said my little piece, shall we go down for breakfast?'

His hand on her arm still held her back. 'Aren't you carrying things a bit far, Roz? In my position . . .'

She looked down at his restraining hand and then back at his face until he released her and stepped back. 'I'm tempted, dear brother-in-law, let's put it that way. But if you start playing fair and square with my sister, I expect I'll be able to withstand the temptation. Ah, I can smell toast and that gorgeous marmalade Eve makes!' and without another word or even a glance at him, she went gaily down the stairs. At the bottom she paused, remembering, and called back, 'Bring my case down, Stephen, there's a dear.'

CHAPTER SEVEN

THE big Cadillac crunched down the gravelled drive and Roz looked about her with pleasure. It mightn't be a very nice-looking house, but the gardens were pleasant, especially at this time of the year. The lawn was smooth and green, the borders were a blaze of colour and Eve's carefully shaped and tended willows wept in a pale, greeny-yellow shower. She breathed a deep sigh of content before she turned in her seat and looked at the driver.

'Stephen told me not to bring you back,' she announced. 'He thinks you're bad for me, so you're persona non grata as far as he's concerned. A bad smell or something nasty in the sewers!'

'I've corrupted you?' Charles gave her a smile as he swung the car out on to the road and accelerated.

'Not me exactly,' she shook her head. 'But you might corrupt Eve. Last night she had all the limelight, and it hurt him. He's not used to being on the fringes.'

'So?' He spared her a glance full of mockery. 'What happens now? Do I stay at the pub in the village or should I travel down early on Wednesday morning?'

Suddenly her bright feeling vanished and she was full of doubts. 'Please yourself, but you're quite welcome at the house. Stephen will behave himself, I've given him his come-uppance and I think now he'll probably take Eve and the kids with him to the States.'

'And you, Roz—are you going to be there on Wednesday, or are you still fighting it?'

'Not fighting any more,' she denied, and then, as a vision of Margery Smith swam before her closed eyes, 'I've thought about it and I think it's the best way. I'm only sorry about the past. I wish it was possible to take it for a walk in the woods, kill it and bury it in an unmarked grave so that it could be forgotten. But it isn't possible, so we'll just have to live with it.' She leaned forward to twiddle the knobs of the radio without result and swore softly as she punched a row of switches with passionate fingers. 'Isn't there a working radio in this mobile palace?'

Charles switched off the de-mister, the rear window heater, the fog lamps and the hazard warning flashers before he guided her fingers to the correct switch. 'That one! It's the aerial. Now try.' And he went back into silence which lasted until he pulled up in the mews.

Roz meanwhile listened to the radio with half an ear while she mused and fretted. This morning the sun had shone to sweep away her indecision, and now she was a mass of 'ifs' and 'buts' again and it wasn't anything to do with her. There were cold waves of distaste emanating from Charles, she could feel them, and the car was full of them. But it was ridiculous! It must be her imagination working overtime. She had made up her mind, Wednesday would be her wedding day; she was just suffering from an attack of nerves. They would be married, and what came after was up to them. Charles seemed to know what he wanted, he had been all for it, so she would have a willing husband if nothing else.

'No secretary?' She made a joke of it as he fitted the key in the lock of his front door.

'No need.' He didn't smile and he stood well away from her as though he was making sure they didn't touch. 'I'm officially on holiday.' He glanced at his watch. 'You go into the kitchen and start on some lunch while I get these films going. I won't be long, and when I come down, we'll have a drink.'

Half an hour later she stood beside him, her jacket removed and the skirt and creamy blouse covered by a brightly coloured, plasticised apron. There was a slight frown on her face because she couldn't understand the change in his behaviour towards her. It was as if, since last night—no, since this morning, he'd become a different person. The cat was back and determinedly walking by itself.

He made no move to touch her, and although she wanted to ask what was wrong, she couldn't. There was a barrier between them and she didn't think he'd hear her through it. She downed the sherry he had poured for her in one gulp and announced surlily that lunch would be ready in fifteen minutes.

Charles merely nodded and went back to his darkroom, his tanks and dishes, and Roz was cross about it. Let him be frozen if he liked! He was evidently in an odd mood, but looking back to their departure from Sussex, she couldn't pinpoint anything she'd said to account for it, she was vicious about shaking the chips free of oil. She wasn't going to put herself out to get him into a better temper!

But she couldn't leave it there, some demon driving her put words in her mouth so that over lunch she speared a couple of golden chips on her fork, added a cube of medium rare steak and looked up at him with angry eyes.

'You've gone back to being "I am" again,' and at his look of polite query, she snorted down her small straight nose. 'Kipling, the cat who walked by himself! What's it like in your wild, wet woods?'

'Lonely.' He was brief, and since Roz could think of nothing else to say, she stuffed her chips and steak into her mouth and chewed stolidly.

Roz spent the afternoon alone in the lounge, curled up on the divan and trying to concentrate on a book, but it wasn't sufficiently interesting to hold her attention and her eyes closed and she drifted off to sleep, to be woken at about five o'clock by Charles.

'Tea?' He proffered a cup.

'Thanks.' She was morose and stupid with sleep. With a grunt, she hoisted herself into a sitting position and demanded to know if they were going out to dinner.

'Too busy.' Charles wasn't just withdrawn, he had all the shutters firmly closed on her. 'We'll have something here. There's plenty of food in the freezer.'

'Omelettes, then.' She became determinedly cheerful even when he wrinkled his nose. 'With cheese and mushrooms, after all, you had steak for lunch. Besides, I can do an omelette just when you're ready for it, I shan't have to call you in the middle of anything crucial.'

'That's reasonable.' His eyes glittered under half closed lids. 'But then you generally are reasonable, aren't you, Roz? You don't act on impulse, do you? Sometimes I think I fool myself when I think there might be more to you than a beautiful face and body and a practical little brain.'

'Have it your way,' she shrugged, and turned away so that he shouldn't see the tears in her eyes.

Except for a break for dinner at eight o'clock, Charles stayed in his darkroom all evening until half past ten when he came downstairs, wiping his hands on a towel which he left draped over the newel post. Roz gave him a dark look and removed it.

'Reasonable and fussy.' The beginnings of a smile glimmered about his eyes and she drew a breath of relief. Whatever it was that had upset him, he was getting over it. Perhaps he was moody by nature, but she looked back over five years and decided against it. He'd never shown any sign of moodiness before.

'A drink and bed,' he announced. 'I can finish that lot by lunch time tomorrow. Oh, by the way,' he took her hand, opened it and slapped a key into her palm, 'your bedroom door. Making assurance doubly sure!'

Roz looked at the key and back at him, saying nothing. She would put the key in the lock but she wasn't going to turn it; that wouldn't be any good and she knew it. If she heard him at the door, if he knocked or even tried the handle, she would be out of bed at the speed of light. She would open the door, haul him inside, and if he wouldn't make love to her, she would make love to him. That was how far she'd sunk, and she wondered what had happened to her lofty morals and her pride.

'Thanks.' Her face was expressionless although her voice was a bit ragged. 'I'll go now. You can get your own drink, I don't want one. See you in the morning.'

Sleep didn't come easily. It hadn't anything to do with the state of her mind nor with the undefinable ache which possessed every bit of her body. It was, she assured herself, because she had dozed all afternoon and had sat watching dreary T.V. all evening. She should have gone for a walk, it would have blown the cobwebs away. The thought of cobwebs upset her further. Suppose Charles called the whole thing off? A few days ago she would have jumped over the moon with joy at the thought, but now all she could see was a future where, like Miss Havisham in *Great Expectations*, she'd remain an old maid and live surrounded by cobwebs.

Therefore, starting right now, she would smile, be her usual composed self; turn away wrath with a soft answer; spin her own web and wait in the middle of it like one of those cannibal spiders, and if Charles stumbled in among her sticky strands, she would eat him alive. With this thought in mind, she turned over on her side, bit the pillow in a spasm of sheer frustration and went to sleep.

So at eight o'clock, she entered the kitchen with a smile on her lips and a pleasant 'good morning'. Charles was making tea with concentration. She watched him as he warmed the pot and carefully measured in the spoonfull.

'You do it properly,' her smile widened. 'I've got into bad habits since I broke my teapot. I make it in a mug, one tea-bag and boiling water. Shall I start on some toast?'

'You're both looking and sounding better this morning.' His glance at her was quizzical.

'So I should.' She didn't mention the half hour she'd spent in the bathroom in front of the mirror while she'd carefully covered up all evidence of strain. 'Yesterday was very restful, I feel better for it, and this morning I'm going shopping.' She glanced at him from under her lashes. 'I'm rather an expensive person, money slips through my fingers. Shall you mind that?'

Charles gave her his devastating smile; it made her catch her breath and wish that it was night-time. 'They say that two can live as cheaply as one, but I've never believed it. I'll make allowances in the budget for increased expenditure and take it from there.'

'Excellent,' she beamed at him. 'I like a man who doesn't haggle over money and who understands the need of a woman for a really good fur coat.'

'Have you enough money?' Now he was being practical. 'You haven't worked for several months . . .'

'Enough,' she assured him. 'Of course, I shall probably be penniless by lunchtime, but you weren't expecting to marry a wealthy woman, were you?' and to cover her embarrassment, she buttered her toast lavishly, spread it thickly with marmalade and bit into it with evident enjoyment.

There had been a shower of rain early that morning, but by the time Roz reached Oxford Street, the pavements were dry and crowded. She went happily from store to boutique to store, rather like a ferret in search of one particular rabbit, and she was still cheerful when after two stores and four boutiques she had found nothing she liked. She liked London, the bustle, the noise, even the crowds. Sussex was all right for a holiday, but she'd grown out of the country life after so long away from it. Now she wouldn't willingly live anywhere else.

In the third store, she found what she was looking for, and she lifted it off the rail with a mute plea that it would be the right size. It didn't look much on the rail, in fact it looked old-fashioned with its demure round collar and pin-tucked bodice, but the material was a fine tussore silk in a soft shade of ivory which suited her better than white. The price tag came in for a close inspection, it made her eyebrows rise but the dress was so suitable. It had a row of self covered little buttons all down the front of the pin tucked bodice, very full sleeves which ended in tight cuffs, a wide, stitched belt to emphasis her narrow waist, and the skirt was full enough to swing round her long legs without looking in the least bulky.

She clutched it to her bosom protectively, as though she was shielding it from other rapacious hands, and hurried to a fitting room. It fitted and the length was right, and Roz breathed a sigh of relief before she glanced at the price tag again. She comforted herself about the enormous expense. This dress would actually save money. She already had shoes, handbags and gloves which would team with it. Perhaps a hat, although she didn't usually wear one, and she went off happily to the millinery department where she chose a small, plain pillbox which she could jazz up if she wished.

At least this outfit wouldn't moulder in the wardrobe for years like Eve's traditional bridal outfit; it was eminently wearable and although it didn't look very weddingy, perhaps if she carried a few flowers—and she wondered if Charles would give her flowers. The fanciful shopping done, she attended to more mundane matters. Some salad stuff for lunch, bread, thinly sliced York ham, and finally she made her way to a tea shop, struggling through the crowds of house-wives out on bargain hunts and teenagers examining the contents of with-it boutiques.

She entered the tea shop with a feeling of relief and dropped the plastic bags containing her purchases on a spare chair while she ordered coffee. While she drank it, she was thinking about the future, what it would be like, how she and Charles would get on together, and she was just making a resolution to put a curb on her tart tongue in the interests of connubial felicity when her reverie was interrupted.

'It's very crowded in here, do you mind if I share your table, Roz?'

Roz looked up, her eyes still slightly glazed with thought, to see Margery Smith at her elbow and smiling down at her in a hesitant way.

'But certainly.' Roz shifted her carrier bags from the spare chair to a point near her feet while under her lashes she surveyed the girl. No, not a girl, a woman. In a better light than there was in Charles' hallway. Margery looked at least thirty, maybe a little older, although it wasn't obvious, not at a cursory glance which was all Roz had ever given her before. A smallish woman, about five foot four, slender and brown-eyed, all this together with her pale hair which had been professionally tipped and streaked to a gilt finish made Margery look younger than her years. In a bad light, she could easily pass for twenty-five. Roz found herself wondering bitchily if the silvery tips and streaks in the immaculate hairdo not only lightened it but concealed the first signs of grey.

Margery sat down thankfully, dropping her own parcels on the floor before she ordered tea. 'Wedding shopping?' she enquired. 'I hope you and Charles are going to be very happy. I'm sure you will,' she added. 'Charles is a wonderful person.'

Roz admired her savoir-faire in stupefied wonder. Margery had an almost little-girl ingenuousness, something quite different from the business efficiency she had displayed when she was Charles' secretary. Away from her desk and appointments book she seemed a different person.

'I'd have loved to come to the wedding,' Margery continued, 'but I have a new job— Charles recommended me for it. I'm with a group medical practice and I can't get away. It's very interesting and I've a lovely little flat, tiny but so convenient. Of course the kitchen's not as nice as Charles'—I designed that myself. Do you like it?'

Roz murmured that it was indeed very convenient, while she decided two things. The first was that it wasn't necessary to hold a conversation, just listen, and the second was that, as soon as she received her first pay cheque from the magazine, she would demolish that kitchen, convenient or not, and have a firm in to build her a new one! Margery meanwhile chattered on.

'I hope you don't mind Charles telling me, he always tells me everything. We've always been so close—well, we would be; we've known each other a long time.'

It all sounded very cosy and intimate, and Roz choked back chagrin. She would have liked to ask 'How close!' She wanted to know the formula for getting Charles' confidence; how to turn the 'cat who walks by himself' into a nice domestic pussy who sat by the fire instead of doing his lone, lorn thing in the wet, wild woods.

None of this showed in her face, though. That part of her was under perfect control. She heard herself make a banal remark which turned the chatter on to what had been going on in London during her absence and Margery became amusingly informative, giving brief, thumbnail sketches of people they both knew and dryly comic descriptions of their activities.

She came away from the tea shop with mixed feelings. She'd learned a very little and it was all confusing. Margery didn't fit in with her idea of a femme fatale, but appearances weren't everything. And Margery did have this cosy relationship with Charles. He'd found her another job and a flat to live in; she wondered acidly if he also paid the rent! The thought of that cosy relationship had her envying like mad because all she shared with him was a hot, desiring thing which, while it screamed for satisfaction, didn't promise warmth or companionship. It was almost too violent to last and when it was sated, what would be left?

Charles was coming down the stairs from the studio when she entered the house, and he raised an eyebrow at her burdens so that she glanced down at the cheerfully coloured plastic carriers, there did seem to be an awful lot of them.

'Spent up?' He made the enquiry with a faintly cynical smile.

'Mmm.' She staggered through the hallway and into the kitchen where she dropped into a chair and kicked her shoes off with a groan of relief. 'I told you I was expensive. Gosh, I could do with a cup of tea!'

'May I see?'

'Isn't it bad luck or something?' She clutched tightly at the yellow bag which contained her dress. 'I remember when Eve was married, everything was whipped out of sight and shrouded in secrecy as soon as Stephen put his finger on the doorbell.'

'Bad luck!' Charles was serious. 'I don't believe in luck, myself, not in marriage.'

'Ah, you go in for the "hard work" and "understanding" theories.' She watched his back as he filled the teapot and arranged the cups and saucers. He was so good to look at that a little bubble of happiness swam up and burst in her throat making her chuckle. 'Do you "understand" me, Charles?'

'Enough.' He brought her tea to where she was sitting. 'Now may I see?'

'Mmm,' but she was curiously reluctant; maybe he wouldn't like it. 'It doesn't look much until it's on, but . . .' she took a sip of tea because her throat had suddenly become tight. 'And there's a hat to go with it, a pillbox and very plain. I thought I might jazz it up a bit. What do you think?' She selected another carrier and took the hat out carefully to perch it on her head.

'No,' he considered it gravely. 'No jazzing, leave it plain, it's better that way. As for the dress,' his finger came out to flick the cameo brooch on her lapel, 'wear that with it, it doesn't need anything else.'

'Are the prints finished?' Roz asked as she tossed the salad for lunch.

'Mmm.' Charles came to stand behind her, putting his arms round her, his hands coming up to cup her breasts. 'I shouldn't be doing this,' he murmured as he nuzzled her neck.

Roz gasped and dropped the salad servers on the counter as the treacherous warmth uncoiled within her. Her legs suddenly became almost too weak to hold her and she leaned back against the warmth of his body for support. 'Why not?' Her question came out as a husky whisper, she was

melting all over and she thought she could feel
him tremble against her. Then, equally suddenly,
she was free and he had stepped back from her.

'I'm behaving myself,' he was wry about it.
'And we're short of time. We'll have lunch and
I'll take you back. If we leave early enough, we'll
miss the rush hour and I should be able to deliver
you at your door in about an hour and a half,
which will give me ample time to get back here.
If we're lucky getting out of London, I just might
manage both journeys while it's still light.'

Roz gasped with dismay. 'Take me back? Aren't
you going to stay?'

'No,' he shook his head. 'I'll come back here
and drive down on Wednesday morning. Leave
it, Roz!' as she started to object. 'You said
Stephen would rather I didn't stay there.'

'But it's not his house . . .'

'Maybe not, but it's his home and Eve's his
wife.' His mouth curved into a small smile. 'I
don't know what you said to twist his arm yesterday, I don't want to know . . .'

'I told him a few home truths, that's all,' she
interrupted defiantly. 'He was overdue for some
of them . . .'

'. . . and I bet he's still smarting!' Charles shook
his head reproachfully at her. 'Leave it to your
sister, my girl, haven't I told you? She's no fool
and she isn't any starry-eyed miss in need of your
care and protection either. I don't approve of
interfering between married couples.'

Roz glared at him. She wasn't loving him now,
he was repulsive, and he had no right to be telling
her what to do! Unthinkingly, she said so, and

added a few other things as well, none of them complimentary, to finish up on a fighting note.

'And if that's the way you think,' she was haughtily furious, 'you needn't bother coming down on Wednesday because I shan't be there. And you can take that,' she threw the yellow plastic carrier and its contents at him, hitting him in the chest with it, 'and you can put it in the dustbin for all I care. I never want to see it again!' And with a crash, she threw the cutlery on the table, followed it with the cruet and fled into the bedroom, slamming the door violently behind her. Once there, she abandoned a lot more restraint and flung herself face down on the bed.

She wasn't crying, there wasn't a tear in her eyes—she had gone too far for that. She would have liked to lie there and scream, but she couldn't. There was the hard, hot lump in her throat which hurt until she thought she'd die of it. She could hardly breathe for the pain of it and her heart was hammering so hard that the blood drummed in her ears. Her first intimation that Charles had joined her was a sharp and quite painful slap on her rear. It was short and salutary, and she squealed with mingled pain and wrath as she rolled over to face him.

'Brute!' she snapped, the fingers of one hand crooked into claws while with the other she massaged her afflicted parts. 'How dare you! Get out of my room!'

'My room,' he corrected as he dropped on the bed beside her and inspected her still suffused face. 'Let that be a lesson, you little harpy!'

'Don't you dare lay a finger on me!' she warned through clenched teeth.

'In your present state, I wouldn't touch you,' he drawled, 'you're a mess!' His eyes slid over her cruelly, making her aware of rumpled clothing, untidy hair and a ladder in her tights which she couldn't account for. 'An unattractive mess,' he added.

The words jolted her into a sitting position from which she could see herself in the mirror and she choked back a groan of despair. He was quite right, she looked wild and unkempt. The things she'd always prided herself on, her cool collectedness, her air of remoteness, her well-groomed look—they were all gone. Beneath her tumbled hair, the face which looked back at her from the mirror was the face of a virago, and the rest of her matched it.

'It's all your fault,' she muttered sulkily as she tried to restore some order to her appearance.

'Perhaps.' Charles stood up and reached out a hand to pull her to her feet. 'Now go and wash and tidy yourself, then we'll eat. After that, I'll take you back to your sister—and,' he put a finger under her chin, tilting her face up to his, 'I'll be at the Register Office at twelve-thirty on Wednesday, that's the day after tomorrow, and you will meet me there, understand?'

'And if I don't?' She was still faintly defiant.

'You will.' He lowered his mouth to hers. There was nothing gentle about his kiss, neither was it mocking, it was cruelly sensual and it lit fires which started to rage through her slender body so that she sagged against him, her arms going about his shoulders, her fingers threading through his hair and her lips parting willingly and hungrily under his.

'That's why!' He had raised his mouth from hers and was looking down into her drugged eyes. 'To put it crudely, darling, you want it as much as I do, and the only way you'll get it is to marry me.' He laughed at her flushed face. 'I've transposed things, my dear. It's usually the woman who insists on marriage, isn't it?'

On Wednesday morning, Roz woke to a clear sky and the sun just tipping over the edge of the Downs. She watched the sky change from a pale primrose to blue and she felt neither happy nor unhappy, she felt numb. Surprisingly, she had slept. When she had gone to bed the previous night, she had been sure that she wouldn't close her eyes, she had even stocked the bedside table with a selection of books to while away the sleepless hours, but she had scrambled herself into bed, switched off the light just in case a miracle happened—and she had slept. She didn't feel any better for it, she was still tired and confused.

Within ten minutes of waking she had lost the numbness, and it was now replaced by a sick, shivering fear. Would Charles come? If he didn't, she would be lost, alone, and nothing that anybody could say would comfort her, she would also be humiliated. If he did come, she would be sick with fright at what she was doing and still humiliated because she would be marrying a man who had just disposed of a mistress with as little thought as he would change his socks.

She slid out of bed and crept downstairs through the silent house to the kitchen where she made herself a cup of tea, loaded it with sugar and drank it while standing by the table. She drained the cup, gagged at the undissolved sweet-

ness in the bottom and up against the pillows ...her. This she
took back upstairs w... went round in ever-de-
bed, she sat there... at the same point every
sipping while ... living
creasing cir...ster Office at half past twelve.
time. Th... hard to realise that it was only two
   It s... since she had been happily certain of where
we... was going and what she was going to do—
...he
well, two weeks and two days, she qualified. In
that short space of time, she had fallen head over
heels in love, and not with a worthy man. Her
pride was in the dust, her morals had proved to
be no better than they need be, she had been
humiliated, slapped and told to keep her nose out of
what was not her business and Charles had sent her
back here alone to wait it out for a day and a half.

She wondered what he'd been doing since she
had last seen him on Monday afternoon. Probably
clearing away the last evidence of his liaison with
Margery Smith, she decided cynically. She could
imagine him going through the house with a fine
tooth comb, dumping the odd pair of laddered
tights, the odd scrap of underwear and the forgotten mac in a cardboard carton together with the
abandoned pair of slippers which had skidded
under the wardrobe and the odd glove crammed
at the back of a drawer.

The sun was quite high when young Freda disturbed her musings.

'Mummy says will you come, she'd come to
you, but Jasper is just woken up and she's feeding
him. Is it true you're getting married, Auntie Roz,
and can I see your veil and dress, please?'

Freda was dressed for school, and the sight of her sturdy little normality drove away the visions of despair.

'You can see my dress.' Roz dragged her face into a smile because upsetting children wasn't in her line, it wasn't fair on them, their minds were too clear-cut, simple and direct to understand, and she had discovered that Freda was amazingly percipient. 'But there isn't a veil, I'm afraid.'

Freda peeped into the wardrobe and sniffed disapprovingly. 'I thought it would be better than that,' she explained, 'but I suppose it's because Charles is shy. All the same, I think it's very unfair. Lots of my friends have been bridesmaids and I wanted to be one too.' And she stumped out of the room registering more disapproval.

Roz slid out of bed, hunted for her slippers which Freda had kicked inadvertently under a chair, wrapped herself in her dressing gown and pattered along to the master bedroom where Eve was putting a clean, full Jasper back in his cot.

'Another dissatisfied customer,' she growled. 'Freda wanted to be a bridesmaid. She's never going to forgive me.'

'Don't be silly.' Eve said soothingly. 'She'll have forgotten it all by tomorrow. She'll have much more fun in school, telling everybody that her Auntie Roz is getting married today.'

Roz's face crumpled into distress. 'Suppose he doesn't come, Eve?'

'Ninny!' Her sister went across to the mirror and peered at her face before making a deplorable grimace at her reflection. 'Of course he'll come.

Stop being stupid. You *know* he will, and I'm very happy for you—and for heaven's sake, take that look of woe off your face! You're going to your wedding, not your funeral.'

'There's a different feeling?' Roz jeered, and then she sobered. 'Why couldn't Freda have come, why must she go to school?'

'Better for her.' Eve waved a white arm. 'Too much excitement, she'd only end up being sick. Honestly, this is the best way, dear. Freda goes to school, the daily is going to stay on to look after Gilly and Jasper—thank the Lord, she's dependable—and we go off and get you married.'

'I don't think I want to be.' Roz was still shrouded in gloom. 'It's all happened in such a rush, I was pushed into it . . .'

'And I know that as well.' Eve moved the pots about on the dressing table. 'Don't be silly, Roz. When have I ever lacked common sense? That face-saving operation of Charles's didn't fool me one little bit. It was kind of him, but it was quite unnecessary. If I looked worried when we caught Stephen trying to kiss you, it wasn't for myself. It was for you. Years ago, I knew you were smitten with Stephen, but I also knew it wasn't anything lasting. I wouldn't have married him if I'd thought you were suffering from anything worse than an overdose of hero-worship, and I know my husband inside out. I love him, but I'm not blind. Sometimes,' she smiled wryly at her reflection, 'he's quite impossible, but as I said, I love him, so it doesn't matter. Food for thought, Roz?'

'I didn't know . . .' Roz sounded uncertain.

'. . . That I knew?' Eve stood up and came to

put her arm about her sister's waist. 'Oh yes, I know all about it, the students, his post-grad girl, the lecture tours, all those adoring women—it's meat and drink to him. He wants fame; he needs admiration, but for love, he comes to me. That's the way it is and that's the way I like it. But it wouldn't do for you.'

Roz let her sister's words sink in and felt a little rage rising. 'You mean it was all unnecessary? The engagement, everything?'

'Charles was seizing an opportunity,' Eve chuckled. 'It's my guess he'd been after you for a long time and there's something between you, a spark—I can't explain it, but it's there.'

'A very basic spark.'

'Don't let's go into that,' Eve smiled widely. 'You'd be surprised at how basic I can be when I'm in the mood! Come and see your wedding present from us instead. I'm fed up with sounding like a maiden aunt, all full of platitudes and advice to "Worried Grey Eyes".'

Roz dutifully enthused about a Minton tea and dinner service in the Haddon Hall pattern. It was what she had always wanted but had never bought because one didn't attempt to house something like that in a flatlet—but having a house to put it in was no reason for getting married! The vicar and his wife had sent a brass carriage clock and somebody, the name was unreadable, had sent some cut crystal wine glasses.

'See?' Eve was on her knees burrowing among wood shavings in the boxes. 'They don't have all the goodies in London. Brighton can come up with excellence as well, when it's pushed.'

'Don't unpack too much,' Roz protested. 'It may all have to go back.'

'Nonsense!' Eve said bracingly. 'Stop being such a silly little fool. This is supposed to be the happiest day of your life, but from the look of you, you're going to dissolve in a puddle of your own misery. I've told you, everything's going to be all right. Do you want some breakfast?'

Roz shuddered at the thought and went upstairs to shut herself in the bathroom. 'And don't be too long,' Eve shouted after her. 'There's somebody besides you wants to get ready. That bathroom is going to be the busiest room in the house today!'

While she was dressing, Charles came, but she didn't see him. He merely left some flowers and picked up her suitcase in which she'd packed enough to last her a week. Eve had been brought a charming spray of fern and red rosebuds while she had a posy, quite a small one of pink roses packed so tightly that they looked like a velvety cushion. There was a card attached to the posy and she opened it eagerly, wanting some sort of assurance, but all it contained was a plain card with 'Don't be late. C.' in Charles' black, precise writing.

After that, she had something else to be nervous about. Suppose she was late, suppose a wheel fell off the car . . . there were a thousand things which could delay her arrival, and from being extremely reluctant to go, she became hysterically certain that something would happen to stop her arriving. But now she didn't let it show. Her face was nicely made up, her dress looked lovely and all she had to do was to pretend there was a camera in front of her all the time. She could be calm and composed for a camera as long as she didn't visualise Charles behind it.

But he *was* waiting and she breathed a sigh of relief as she stumbled into the Register Office for the short and very simple ceremony, and afterwards, at the hotel, she drank a glass of sherry and two glasses of champagne in quick succession, which enabled her to smile back at happy faces without throwing her posy on the floor and asking what everybody was so damn happy about. Didn't they realise she had made a mess of her life?

There was plenty of finger food to mop up the champagne and in pride of place was a wedding cake, and Roz found herself wondering who Eve had bullied over the phone to get it ready in such a hurry. It was little thoughts like these which kept her sane, although the feel of Charles' hand over her own was warm and comforting and when he wasn't holding her hand, his arm was about her waist. Gradually she started to relax, to notice what was going on and who was there.

'All done.' Charles had seated her in the car and was driving out of Brighton, on the London road. 'Do you like it?' He nodded at the wedding ring on her finger.

Roz looked down at it wonderingly. She hadn't even looked at it. 'It's heavy.' She examined the wide, thick band of gold and some of her waspishness returned. 'It feels like a fetter, I wonder you bothered. Why didn't you invest in a pair of gold-plated handcuffs?'

'They wouldn't have suited you.' There was a glimmer of a smile about his face and she relapsed into a silence which lasted for the next ten miles.

'And what about a honeymoon?' she demanded when the atmosphere in the car became almost more than she could bear.

'Not possible at the moment.' He didn't look at her. 'I've a bit of work to clear up before I'm free.'

'You mean you aren't sitting there with two tickets to the Bahamas in your pocket?' she snapped bitingly. 'No honeymoon suite booked at the Bahamas Hilton or whatever it's called?'

'No, Roz,' he answered tranquilly, 'there's no sugar on this pill. Maybe later, in a week or so's time, we can get away for a few days, but until then, we'll stay at my place and get to know each other a bit better.'

'Our place,' she corrected firmly, and then to change the subject, 'Did you see our wedding presents and the cake? I don't know how Eve arranged it so quickly.' She was chattering in a tone of false gaiety, but it was all she could think of doing. Talking about trivialities, treading warily and trying not to think about the future; she was even beginning to wish that this drive could go on for ever. But of course it wouldn't. She wanted to reach out and touch him, but she couldn't do that either, something inside her was keeping her rigid in the seat with her hands tightly clasped in her lap. She was almost surprised when he pulled off the road into the car park of a restaurant.

'Tea.' He was firm as he hauled her out of the car. 'You look as though you could do with it.'

When they arrived at the mews cottage, Charles

brought in her suitcase, dumped it on a stand by the bedroom window and then vanished into the bathroom. He didn't occupy it for very long, but he made his presence felt. As soon as he appeared, Roz fled into the steamy interior and ran a bath as hot as she thought she could stand it, liberally splashing in bath essence. But even this couldn't overpower the sharp sweetness of his masculine cologne, the room was full of it, and she lowered herself into the bath with a moan of discontent. She was as nervous as a cat and she had been relying on the bath to help her to relax, but somehow she didn't think it would work.

But gradually, as she lay in the scented water, the chill went out of her body and her sick trembling passed, so that by the time she had scrambled out of the water, given herself a quick rub down to remove most of the moisture and wrapped herself in a large towelling robe which she found hung up on the bathroom door, she was feeling warm and a bit more able to cope. She pattered back to the bedroom. She wasn't confident, but she had re-found the courage which would help to disguise her nervousness.

Charles turned from the mirror where he was fiddling with his tie. 'No,' he said as she sprang the locks of the suitcase, 'don't change. Wear the dress you were married in for this evening. It suits you,' and he nodded to where she had left it lying across the end of the bed.

'The arbiter of fashion!' she scolded. 'That dress is a bit prim and old-fashioned and most of the girls I know wouldn't be seen dead in it. I bought it for the wedding and nothing else. It doesn't match up to my image.'

'Change your image,' he shrugged. 'Or let me change it for you. I like that dress, and I'm not often wrong.'

'So you like it!' She shrugged and pushed him aside to sit at the dressing table. 'Now may I have your room instead of your company? I've my face to do, and for that I need peace and quiet, not to mention a steady hand. In other words, privacy.'

When he was gone, she stripped off the robe, inserted herself into fresh underwear and sat in her slip before the mirror, her hair held back with a wide, soft band. She didn't need privacy for her face at all. Charles had always had this thing about heavy make-up, he was continually prattling about skin texture, so she contented herself with a smear of light foundation, a slightly darker lipstick and then whisked a powder puff over it all before she slipped the dress over her head and wriggled it down over her hips.

They were going out to dinner and she hoped Charles had chosen somewhere very bright, very noisy so that she couldn't hear herself think. She didn't want to think, she wanted to be mindless and without a thought in her head. Charles' choice of a restaurant didn't come in that category, it was quiet and select, the maître d'hotel and his team of waiters were all of the old school, hushed, reverential and efficiently understanding, but the food was superb and she was so hungry that conversation took a second place. In any case, she and Charles had nothing to talk about, she reasoned it out while she was dealing with wafer-

thin slices of delicious duck and pork pâté, worked
her way steadily through a Chateaubriand steak
garnished with artichoke hearts and finished up
with an apricot soufflé.

She and Charles had very little in common. They
got on very well on opposite sides of a camera and
they would probably be very good together in bed.
She banished this thought almost as soon as it
occurred to her and took a deep draught of dry red
wine to wash away the last traces of it.

Back at the house, she turned to him. 'Now, I
suppose you want your everlasting tea. I don't
want any, I'm too tired and I'm going straight to
bed.' But when he entered the bedroom some
twenty minutes later, she was still at the window,
looking out over the small back garden. It was a
warm night, but she had started to shiver again,
but not with cold. It was sheer nerves! She had
undressed, taken a perfunctory shower, scrambled
her still damp body into a nightie and had been,
for the last ten minutes, concentrating all her attention on the moonlit little garden.

It wasn't much to look at or even much of a
garden, only a small square of grass surrounded
by a narrow, neat border of flowers and with a
tree of some sort, it was too dark to tell what, in
the corner. But there was room on that small plot
of grass for a garden swing hammock in the
summer, something bright with a flower-printed
canopy in cream and red. She was thinking about
anything, anything which came into her head just
to keep her mind on mundane subjects, and all
because she was shy! She snorted in self-derision
as Charles came into the room, dropping cufflinks

on to the dressing-table and making a neat pile of the loose change from his pockets.

'What's wrong, Roz?' he enquired, and there was amusement in his voice. 'You're behaving like a frightened virgin.'

She swallowed to clear her throat of the huge lump which was occupying it, but even so, her muttered answer was hardly audible to start with, although her voice strengthened as she went on.

'Because that's what I am, and what's wrong with being a frightened virgin? It's not criminal, is it?'

He came towards her, she felt his arms about her trembling body, turning her within their circle to face him. He tipped up her face and in the moonlight she thought she saw an almost tender smile about his mouth. The tears she had been wanting to shed ever since early that morning welled up in her eyes, spilled over and ran down her cheeks. 'Oh, Charles,' she sniffed inelegantly and tried to steady her voice. 'I don't know what to say, I don't know what to do, don't you understand? I don't *know*. I don't even know if we've done the right thing.'

She burrowed her wet face against his shirt, seeking wildly for something, she didn't know what, and the arms around her tightened.

'Get your face out of my shirt, Roz,' his voice was husky. 'I want to kiss you,' and suddenly she was frightened no longer. The cold shivering had passed and she was filled with warmth and a wanton sweetness which made her weak. She raised her face and felt his mouth drift across her eyelids and over her cheeks, almost as though he was wiping away the traces of tears, and then he found her willing mouth. And then it no longer mattered that she didn't know; she felt his hands at her shoulders, undoing the ties which held her nightgown in place, and when it fell in a huddle about her feet, she stepped out of it to let him catch her up in his arms and bear her away to the bed.

She whimpered softly, but his mouth stifled her cry as together they scaled heights that were almost unbearable in their beauty and then fell off the top together, in each other's arms, into a deep warmth of the sweetest satisfaction she had ever known.

A grey dawn woke her, that and the movement of something heavy against her breast.

'You're not still frightened, Roz?' Charles murmured against her breast, his warm breath tickling, caressing her soft skin.

'No.' She made vague, ineffectual motions which should have pulled the sheet closer about her to cover her nakedness but which didn't succeed. 'It's just that I'm not accustomed to this sort of— of intimacy. It might take me some time to get used to it,' but even as she was speaking, she was aware of her traitorous body inviting him. There was a slackness about her limbs and she could feel her breasts grow taut under the assault of his mouth. His unshaven chin rasped against her flesh and she didn't care. Nothing mattered except making him happy, making them both happy. The breaths she drew were ragged as passion and wildness swept over her again, making her soft and malleable in his hands. And this time there was no hesitancy and her inarticulate murmurs held no thread of fear.

When she next wakened, the clock was showing half past eight, and she hoisted herself on her elbow to examine his sleeping face. He looked much younger asleep even with the shadow of a beard on his chin. She put out a hand to stroke it and felt the faint rasp on her fingertips. Charles' dark hair flopped over his forehead, his mocking eyes were closed—she was astounded at the length and silkiness of his eyelashes—and his mouth was less firm, more curved and contented. She bent her head to lay her cheek against his, feeling the arm about her tighten. This was hers, and nobody could ever take it away from her. If she died right here, right this minute, she'd have known what it was to be completely, wildly, ecstatically happy.

Her thoughts drifted to the days, weeks, months, perhaps years ahead, and she frowned. Would it always be like this? Was she going to be like Eve after all? Would she be content with her share so that she could excuse the odd peccadillo, dismiss it with an understanding smile as Eve dismissed Stephen's falls from grace? Could she be content with being a loved but occasionally betrayed wife? Awarding herself so many points for her husband, her house and her children, if she had any, and making a sum of those points and being satisfied if the total came only close to top marks?

The little bedside clock pinged out its alarm and she relaxed, closing her eyes and making her breathing even and steady as she felt him stir.

'Do you want a cup of tea, darling?' Charles

murmured in her ear and then gently bit the lobe to wake her up.

'Mmm.' She turned over on her stomach, burying her hot face in the pillows. 'Lovely,' she muttered.

'And after that, you get up.' He was ruefully apologetic. 'There's a girl coming at half past ten this morning, another entry in the Baby Care stakes. I told you I had work to do.'

'Make a mess of it,' she advised, the words coming out slightly muffled because she hadn't raised her face from the pillows.

'And ruin my reputation? No, Roz—and I need you about. She's new to me and I prefer to have another female in evidence.'

'Where's your secretary?' she grumbled through a stifled yawn. 'Can't she go and do the chaperon bit?'

He sat down on the side of the bed beside her to push his feet into a pair of casual slip-ons. 'I can't afford a secretary *and* a wife,' he said blandly as he stood up.

'Oh lord!' Still she didn't raise her face from the pillows. 'I've married a pauper, I knew there was a snag in it somewhere. That damn car is no more than the outward show of an empty bank balance—and I suppose this house is mortgaged to the hilt?'

There was no reply to this and when she looked up, he had gone. She heard the chink of cups and saucers from the kitchen, the metallic rattle of teaspoons, and grimaced. Love and romance were over for the time being. Charles had gone back to work, he hadn't even waited to hear what she said. Dedication! That was his watchword, and he was now, presumably, in his working hours. She wished she could compartmentalise her emotions in the same way!

When he came back in with her tea, he was already washed, shaved and dressed. Her eyes flickered over him appreciatively as she took the cup and saucer he proffered; he noticed the glance and leaned forward to place a rather restrained kiss on her mouth.

'And I advise you to go and do the same,' he murmured as he raised his head. 'Shower and dress, I mean. The daily arrives at half past nine and she'll think I've married a slut if she finds you still in bed.'

Roz found, over the next two weeks, that the transition from photographer's model to photographer's wife was very painful and that without the easing-in period which would have come with a conventional honeymoon, there was nothing to cushion the bump. Charles was fussy about time. His appointments were made and he expected them to be kept to the minute. Most of them were, but occasionally a young, wide-eyed girl turned up half an hour late, and without blinking an eyelash blamed it all on the secretary for having booked in the wrong time, producing as proof a scribbled figure in a scrappy diary.

Roz became cross when this happened. It was a ploy she had used once or twice herself when she had first started, but she had never been allowed to get away with it. Charles didn't blame her—well, not very much. Also he was fussy about the time and duration of his breaks, and Roz, sitting in the lounge and busy with pencil and paper, sketching clothes, was inclined to become engrossed with her own affairs so that he had to make his mid-morning tea himself and his lunches were frequently a disaster, either ready too late or too early for his implacable idea of a timetable.

The second week in July was a particularly disastrous time. Roz had been to see her editor, who was more than pleased with the photographs of Roz in a country setting and who now wanted an outline of her first article to read and correct for content, after which she wanted the whole thing so that it could be read again, corrected again and proofed before the September edition of the magazine went to print.

Charles, meanwhile, was busy with three models and a hamper of clothing from a large chain store. They were good, well finished clothes, based on what the chain store's experts thought the autumn and winter look would be. They weren't yet on the market, in fact everybody, including Charles was treating them as one big secret and Roz thought she ought to be entitled to a preview.

The girls arrived, one to do the teenage thing, another girl who would portray what the gear would look like on the twenty-five to thirty-five-year-old and a more mature woman for the 'over forties' look. She knew the two older girls and greeted them with pleasure, explaining her presence with a laughing, 'I'm married now and out of the business,' and the teenager turned on the stairs to look down on her.

'Oh yes, I heard about it from a friend, To Charles, isn't it? You should be so lucky!'

Roz scored through their names in the appointments book with such force that her ballpoint nearly went through the paper. Lucky! Was that what they really thought? It was a pity they didn't know the truth. That she spent most of the day by herself while Charles was upstairs snapping away merrily and that most of her evenings were nearly as lonely because although he wasn't upstairs clicking his abominable shutter, he was there, locked in a darkroom, and she was alone downstairs.

She was beginning to feel very sorry for herself, and when Charles refused to give her copies of the chain store photographs, she felt more than sorry for herself, she felt a definite sense of ill-usage.

'But it would save so much time,' she protested, getting heated and letting it show.

'You know better, Roz.' Charles wasn't even taking her seriously. 'The clothes are a secret, the materials used are equally under wraps and they aren't being shown until August when the store is launching a publicity campaign.'

'But the magazine doesn't come out until September,' she argued. 'I shan't be stealing their thunder.'

'Then go and ask for permission.' He was brusque, treating her almost as though she was a petulant child.

'Pig!' she stormed, and went off to bed leaving the dinner dishes unwashed and the kitchen in a dreadful mess. She pretended to be asleep when he came into the bedroom, lying on her side, turned away from where he would be and breathing slowly and deeply; making each breath even and keeping her eyes firmly shut. But he wasn't deceived, he slid into bed and his hands came to turn her over.

'Stop pretending, Roz. You don't fool me,' and his hands were soothing, caressing and seducing so that she found herself tumbling into his arms with a wanton ferocity, but it wasn't enough, she told herself when, sated, they lay with arms entwined about each other. There should be more to marriage than this driving need; there should be warmth, understanding and companionship, and so far, sadly she went over the score, there had been little of those more enduring qualities.

CHAPTER NINE

By the beginning of the last week in July, Roz had got her new life in order, and although the promised honeymoon had been delayed once more, she was not overmuch sad about it, but the time was hanging heavy on her hands. The transition from a busy, sometimes hectic life to the slower pace at the mews cottage was a bit traumatic, but she enjoyed not having to rush about with a suitcase full of changes and a bulging make-up bag.

'When's that honeymoon coming off?' she demanded of him. Eve had phoned that she and the children were going off to the States with Stephen and Roz found herself afflicted by a wanderlust.

'Not this month.' Charles tossed a letter across to her. '*They* want photographic Christmas cards and it's the opportunity of a lifetime. You wouldn't have me miss it, would you?'

She glanced at the signature at the bottom of the piece of heavy paper and shook her head. 'My, my,' she marvelled while she buried her hopes. 'You'll soon be up among the greats, taking your place beside Lichfield, Bailey and Snowdon.'

Charles looked at her thoughtfully. 'It bothers you, the quiet life?'

'N-no——' She heard herself sounding not very sure, so she expanded the theme. 'You know very well that I never went in for a mad round of gaiety, it wouldn't have done. You'd have been turning up your nose when you printed a close-up of me. Let me see if I remember your rules.' She gazed up at the kitchen ceiling and pursed her lips. 'Early to bed and early to rise, no smoking and the minimum of alcohol; and then there was the ban on rich food which successfully eliminated all those dinners I was invited to partake of at nightclubs and such. I've got it right, haven't I? I ought to, you told me often enough.'

'So I did,' he grinned, 'and it was successful, wasn't it? You still look as good as you did five years ago.'

'But,' she raised her eyebrows, 'I thought you said I was passée, that you would have to fog prints. Wasn't I haggard and haunted . . .?'

'You're still haunted, Roz.' His glance became acutely professional. 'It's in your eyes, I think. Can't you bury those memories?' His eyes searched her face and she flushed under his scrutiny. 'No, you can't, can you?' Under his heavy lids, his eyes glittered darkly. 'Damn you, Roz, why can't you forget? It's like living with a ghost between us. Even in bed I can feel the bloody thing there!' He rose and moved catlike to the door, pausing with his hand on the knob. 'Get rid of it, Roz!' He was vehement. 'It's all in the past. Write it off as experience.'

When he had gone, slamming the door behind him, she poured herself another cup of tea and sat quietly drinking it. His behaviour didn't upset her, she had worked with him for too long for that. Any small detail which wasn't quite right was enough to send him into a torrent of caustic comment. What did worry her was the fact that he seemed to know how the memory of his long affair with Margery would keep intruding into her mind. A lot of the time, she hardly thought about it, but occasionally it hit her, making her feel uncertain despite herself.

She loved him and she had told herself that she could take anything in her stride, but this wasn't anything. A few brief affairs she could ignore, brush them aside with a shrug. What man of thirty-five or so had ever behaved like a Trappist monk except a Trappist monk? She was practical about it, she wouldn't have enjoyed inexperienced fumbling; as far as lovemaking was concerned, Charles led and she followed, and she preferred to be led by an expert.

But a man who had lived with the same woman for five years, that was something different again. It was like marrying a widower or a divorcee, there would always be that ghost lurking in the background. He would have memories and in moments of stress he would be comparing life with her to the life he had experienced with another woman. Roz sighed as she imagined Margery trotting about the house, working in the kitchen, making herself comfortable in the lounge and . . . the bedroom was the worst. Sometimes, not often but sometimes during the night, Roz could even feel the woman lying between them. Hadn't Margery told her that she and Charles had always been close? How much closer could you get than that!

Once she had been tempted to go and see

Margery, assess the opposition, maybe find out a little more, but a few moments' reflection made her realise that such a course of action would be stupid. What could she say? She could hardly walk into a strange woman's house and demand to know intimate details of things which, properly, weren't her concern.

So it wasn't really *her* ghost, her memories which were causing the slight friction between her and Charles. It was Charles' ghost, a phantom Margery who had known him so long and to whom he always told everything! How did he suppose she could get rid of it? That was for him to do and in the sensible way. All he had to do was to tell her about it, to tell her that it was all over, that he now loved her, Roz, and that Margery meant nothing to him any more. But he never spoke of it, and she was too proud to ask questions.

The daily woman tramped into the kitchen and Roz escaped as soon as possible, but not before she'd been treated to a lengthy list of complaints which spanned everything from corns and bunions to the price of pork chops. She murmured sympathetically at the price of tinned dog food and details of a visit to the chiropodist as she edged towards the door, and once through it, she fled to the hallway to consult the appointments book.

Charles had two this morning, a girl whom she knew very well who did Scottish knitwear; she was coming at ten o'clock and there was another girl for a lipstick advertisement at eleven-thirty. She supposed he was quite prepared, he rarely forgot anything to do with his work, but it was safer to take no chances, so she ran lightly up the stairs to the studio to remind him.

'Knitwear at ten, lipstick at eleven-thirty.' His assistant hadn't arrived yet and Roz watched him assembling a backdrop; a misty blue sky with a bit of a mountain, purple with heather. 'A piper in the background would be effective,' she murmured, and skittered back downstairs before he threw something at her.

The knitwear girl arrived promptly and chatted blithely as she struggled in with a small suitcase and two long cardboard boxes. 'My twice yearly stint for the classic look, and this time there's an addition. The firm's doing a line in sheepskin coats and jackets, they're gorgeous—feel!' She lifted the lid of one of the boxes and directed Roz's fingers among the tissue paper wrappings.

'Mmm.' Roz fingered the soft skins appreciatively. 'Lovely.'

'And very good value. Remember the name if you're buying, and don't forget to write to the firm and tell them it was me who recommended them. You'd look dishy in the coat; it's out of this world. Have you finished altogether, Roz? I heard a rumour about you and a magazine, is it true?'

'Very true, Maggie.' Roz grinned as she checked the name off in the book. 'Remember, you write to *my* firm and tell them how much help I've been in making a better and more beautiful *you*!'

There were no appointments after lunch and Charles was incommunicado having locked himself away in a darkroom to start developing the negatives

from this morning's work, so Roz put on a light
mac and went for a walk; she felt she needed the
fresh air and exercise. She wouldn't be missed,
and she dawdled happily along Cheyne Walk,
watching the river traffic, admiring the houses, as
she always did and the ripples of sunlight on the
surface of the water. She bought some fresh
flowers for the house and arrived back at four
o'clock. The telephone was ringing as she crossed
the threshold, but by the time she had closed the
door and picked up the handset, whoever had
been trying to get through had stopped trying, and
all she heard was the steady 'Brr' of an open line.

She made a mental note to attack Charles once
more on the advisability of having an extension in
the studio. Her previous attempts had met with
no success because he disliked even the thought of
being interrupted—and after making him a pot of
tea and delivering it to the door of the darkroom, she
hurried off to get on with her task of the moment
which was the housing of her Minton china.

Eve had rung during the first week in July,
bubbling with enthusiasm. 'We're all off to the
States, we're flying, and Freda's over the moon
with joy!' Her voice had been lilting with laughter. 'Isn't it fabulous! And Stephen's told me it's
all due to you. You assured him that I'd go without thinking twice about it. He's always hesitated
about asking me before in case I refused.' Roz
had smiled to herself grimly. So that was how her
brother-in-law had explained it away! She gave
him full marks for subtlety, and then she had
listened to the rest of Eve's communication, which
was of more importance to her. 'By the way, I've

had your wedding presents boxed up and I've been in touch with a firm of carriers, so you should be receiving them next week some time.'

Roz had groaned aloud. 'Impetuous—I was going to ask you to hang on to them for a while, I've nowhere to put the china. Couldn't you . . .' She had changed her mind about asking favours; Eve would be busy getting ready for the trip, she wouldn't want to be bothered altering arrangements. 'No, I suppose you couldn't.'

'Couldn't what?' At her sister's query, Roz made her explanation as short as possible.

'The thing is—I've been hunting for a dresser, one of the old type and not an antique. They're not scarce, I've found several, but the prices they want for them! You'd think they were Georgian, not chuck-outs from Victorian and Edwardian kitchens.'

'A dresser?' From being excited, Eve became calm and helpful. 'Is that all you want? What about the dresser from here, that is if it hasn't already been chopped up for firewood. Would that do you? I've rearranged the kitchen, had a few new units in along that wall, and the old thing doesn't go with wipe-clean melamine. Do you want it? Because if you do, the carrier can bring it up with the other things.'

Roz had visualised the dresser, not a real antique but definitely better than the ones she had seen. It had been sandpapered down and re-varnished, so it was quite presentable, and it would be free!

'Yes, please,' she took up the offer without

further thought. 'Don't let anybody chop it up, it'll be ideal for the china.'

'And hell to dust and polish,' Eve had gurgled, and then gone back to details of the trip to the States.

After she had hung up, Roz had gone around the little house looking for some place to put the thing. It wouldn't fit into the lounge and it would be an anachronism in the kitchen among the modern units, but there was the garden room, a subterranean place which overlooked the minute garden which was on a lower level than the pavement at the front of the mews.

Charles had been using it as a storeroom, she discovered when she went investigating. There were cartons full of plastic jars of chemicals, more cartons containing photographic paper together with a whole pile of discarded junk, and Roz had set to with a sense of purpose; she had only a week to get the place ready.

The cartons were taken up to the attics, the junk was disposed of—she had paid the council refuse collectors to take most of it away—and then she had cleaned the room thoroughly before painting the ceiling and walls with white emulsion. The floor of the room was terrazzo tiles, chipped here and there, but a few rugs would cover the worst areas and she would buy new curtains for the wide window and the French one which looked out over the pocket handkerchief of a lawn.

The dresser had come in two pieces, so there was no difficulty in getting it down the narrow stairway at the very back of the hallway, and now, after her walk, she intended unpacking the china and arranging it. She was hopeful that, if she called Charles down when she had finished, the sight of a lonely dresser with its burden of Minton in an otherwise unfurnished room might spur him into furnishing the place properly so that it could be used instead of wasted.

A glance at her watch assured her that she had at least an hour before she need start preparations for dinner, and armed with a screwdriver she opened the door at the top of the stairs and went down to attack the packing case. It was a stout wooden one; Eve, the complete housewife, believed in doing things properly; the screwdriver wasn't all that effective and Roz broke a fingernail before at last she prised the lid from the box. The wood shavings in which the china was packed made an awful mess, but she comforted herself that it would all sweep up easily from the tiles and she spent a happy hour, head down in the packing case and with wood shavings and sawdust flying in all directions as she burrowed and tenderly removed each plastic-wrapped piece. Finally it was all out, and she gasped at the time it had taken. Over an hour, and she was nowhere near finished yet!

'You'll have to wait till tomorrow,' she told the pile of plates, and as she passed the box she gave it a hearty kick and tossed the bent screwdriver in among the sawdust; after which she mounted the narrow stairs to let herself into the shadowed dimness of the back of the hallway to look to where Charles was standing with a weeping Margery plastered closely against him, her arms about his shoulders and her small, pale hands grasping and clutching convulsively at the fine silkiness of his black polo-necked sweater. She was sobbing something about it all being a mistake and Charles was comforting her in a very expert way.

Roz watched him lower his dark head to lay his cheek tenderly against Margery's tear-wet one; she heard his comforting murmur of a promise that everything would be all right, and she stood there in the shadows woodenly while everything inside her turned to ice and her hands clenched until the nails bit into her palms. She gripped her lip between her teeth to stop herself crying out as he led Margery into the lounge with a protective arm about her shoulders, and when the door closed behind them, she came back to some sort of life. She walked steadily down the hall, picked up her mac and her bag and let herself out through the door, closing it quietly behind her.

She felt no hurt, she was too frozen and numb, and she allowed some sort of instinct to take her footsteps to the Tube station. Her fingers searched in her bag automatically, found her purse and pushed enough money across the counter. She watched them doing it, surprised that they could even hold the coins, and she let the same instinct take her through the railway station, purchase a ticket, locate the correct platform and climb aboard the train.

It was the instinct of a wild, wounded animal, the dull necessity to get back to its lair, lick its wounds and lie down quietly to live or die as the fates disposed. The animal would make no noise on its homeward journey and neither did Roz. It was beginning to hurt now, but the hurt was too painful to make a fuss about it. When she was safe, perhaps she would scream with the pain of it, but it would be in a private place where nobody would hear her. At present, she was still too numb and frozen to feel anything but the need to hide.

By the time she left the train, some more of the numbness had worn off so that she could unclasp her stiff fingers from her bag, take out her purse and scrabble through the contents, the few notes and the handful of coins it contained. It was the remains of her housekeeping money and the bag was one she kept for shopping; it contained her purse, her key-ring and nothing else except a week-old shopping list. But there was enough to get her home.

In the taxi, she shook herself alive to be practical, forcing her mind to work on survival lines. Eve and her family had been gone for three days; there would be food in the freezer, dry goods in the cupboards . . . She leaned forward and tapped the partition, asking the driver to set her down at the end of the lane which led to the farm. To buy bread at this time of night was impossible, but she could buy milk at the farm and order a daily delivery.

Deliberately, she kept her mind on mundane things to stop thinking about anything else, because once she let her mind wander, she knew that she would start screaming. She would have to switch on the electricity, perhaps notify the police that she was here—Stephen would have told them that the house would be empty and if there were lights showing, somebody was bound to ring the local station. People in villages were

like that. They were kind, thoughtful and interfering! She wouldn't have to switch on the
power line because the freezer ran off that and
Eve wouldn't have switched that off, not after
laboriously filling it with garden produce. She
would also have to turn on the stop tap to get
water ... And she left the farm with a pint
bottle of milk tucked under her arm, to take the
footpath across the fields which would bring her
out on to the road within a hundred yards of the
house.

The empty house felt cold and bleak. It wasn't
a home any more, it was just a lot of empty rooms
and passages, all waiting for somebody to come
and live in them, to bring them alive. Roz groped
around in the kitchen to find a box of matches and
wasted a great many of them while she sorted
out which fuses had been removed. Stephen, she
thought savagely, was too thorough. It wasn't
enough for him to cut off the current, he had to
take out the fuses as well!

The kitchen was clean and neat and the key to
the stop tap was in its usual place in the cupboard
under the kitchen sink; she got it out and went to
wrestle with the iron cover which protected the
tap, breaking another fingernail in the process.
That made two in one day; she would have to get
busy with an emery board tomorrow. Her mind
was still rigidly running on its practical lines as
she went upstairs to switch on the immersion
heater. She would go back down to the kitchen
and have a glass of milk, by that time, with luck
there would be enough hot water for a bath. There
were aspirin in the bathroom cabinet and she

would take two of them with a cup of tea after she'd had a bath.

The milk was icy cold and she smiled to herself sourly as she sat at the kitchen table drinking it. She hadn't managed this very well. She should have taken her time, thought a bit more and brought some things with her, a change of underwear at least—but it didn't really matter. She could wash out her things and leave them to dry overnight. Nothing mattered, not now; not with Charles putting things right after he and Margery had made the mistake of splitting up.

Roz put that thought out of her mind as she went through the routine she'd planned, she was dry eyed although she thought her heart was truly breaking, it hurt so much. A glass of milk; upstairs to raid the linen cupboard for towels and an old robe of Eve's, then a tepid bath because the immersion heater hadn't been on long enough and back down to the kitchen to make a cup of tea, swallow the two aspirin and count her money.

She hitched her feet under her on the chair and covered them with the end of the robe, they were bare and cold because Eve's slippers were too small for her, and she spread the contents of her purse on the table top and looked at it ruefully. There wasn't a lot left, the taxi from Brighton had been expensive, but it would be enough for quite a while. She wasn't planning on going anywhere for several days. She didn't need much, some bread perhaps, the milk was going to be delivered and Eve's cupboards were well stocked besides the hoard of tinned goods which her sister called emergency food. Tomorrow she would

open a can of soup, if she felt like eating anything.

Later on, she would go down to the bank in
Brighton, get her balance transferred and a new
cheque book. Until then she would manage with
what she had and what was in the house.

On the way upstairs, she leaned over the banisters and took the phone off the hook, then she
thought again and replaced it. It was better to
have a phone ringing and not answered than to
have somebody getting an engaged tone from an
empty house, and she didn't want any visitors,
not until she had thought it all out and decided
how she was going to act. It wasn't any good
trying to make any plans, not yet.

She found sheets and pillowcases in the airing
cupboard and made up her bed to slip under the
duvet, only to start trembling with the shock of
her loss, but finally the tears came and she wept
with deep, hurting sobs which shook her slender
frame. But that didn't matter either. She was
quite alone, there was nobody to hear her.

Some time during the night, she was wakened
by muted peals of thunder. The south of England
had been enjoying a mini heatwave and the air
had been growing steadily more oppressive, but
now the fine spell had broken, and Roz listened
as the thunder grew louder and nearer. She didn't
know what time it was, her watch had stopped
and the electric clock in the kitchen wasn't telling
the correct time, but it was still dark, and she lay
in bed listening to the rising wind and the first
spatters of rain against the window.

Now was the time to be practical, now she was

quiet and could make plans—but her mind wasn't ready to plan. It insisted on going back over the last two months. That was all it was, two months, and she should have thought about this before she had hurled herself into marriage. It wasn't as if she was a teenager, she was a woman of twenty-five and she should have known better.

She and Charles had been friendly for five years, but apart from his frequent attempts to get her into bed, which alternated with long periods when he treated her as just another one of the girls, they had never been all that close. There was that damn word again. He had been close to Margery! She should have known that his be-haviour, after he came down to Sussex, wasn't normal. Charles was the bachelor type, the cat by himself—had his insistence on marriage been to teach Margery a lesson? Mad, weird ideas flocked into her mind. He and Margery had split up and he wanted to prove to the world and himself that he didn't care. To do it, he'd used Roz in much the same way that she replaced sugar with sac-charine if she wanted to lose a bit of weight.

Margery was the sugar, she was saccharine, as sweet but with a bitter taste at the back of it. Charles hadn't really liked it, so when the chance came to revert to his sugar ... This started her crying again, and she thumped the pillow in des-peration as the tears continued to fall, and finally she fell asleep with a damp feeling under her cheek.

CHAPTER TEN

Roz woke early after a short, heavy sleep. She woke feeling dull, headachy, lethargic and hopeless—so hopeless that she wondered why the sun should be shining. The thunderstorm of the night was over and the rain had cleared, now the sun was up and sparkling on wet leaves. By rights, it should have been overcast, grey, sodden with a chill dampness; as utterly miserable as she felt herself.

She ached all over with wanting Charles, her eyes were hot and puffy with weeping, the lids felt heavy and her head was solid. She lay still for several minutes, wallowing in grief, and then struggled out of bed to wrap herself in Eve's old robe; at least she wouldn't have to queue for the bathroom this morning and the water would be good and hot.

She stood under the shower, uncaring that her hair was getting wet, letting the needle jets play on her back until she felt some life returning to her numbed body. Then she towelled herself briefly, wrapped up once more in the robe and pattered downstairs on bare feet to make a cup of tea. She set out a mug, tossed a tea bag into it and switched on the kettle before she realised she had drunk the whole of her pint of milk last night. There were faint rumblings from her stomach to remind her that she'd had nothing solid since lunch the previous day, and she flung open the cupboard doors to inspect the contents.

There was a variety of cereals, but she dismissed them. She didn't want anything really, the tea perhaps and a glass of milk which would slip easily past the hard, hurting lump in her breast, she'd gag on anything else, and she made her way to the back door where the milkman always left the bottles.

She was bitterly amused to find that she'd not only locked it, she had also shot both bolts, top and bottom. With a bit of a struggle, she pushed the bolts back, turned the key and opened the door on to the red-tiled porch—and there, sitting beside the milk bottles, was Charles, a leather jacket flung across his shoulders against the morning chill.

He looked like a big black cat as he rose lithely to his feet, picked up the bottles in one hand and held out the other to her. Like an automaton, Roz put her hand in his and followed as he led her into the house.

'I told you, Roz, don't you remember? Nobody walks out on me, and certainly not my wife.' He said it quietly in a conversational tone as he put the bottles on the table and leaned over to switch off the kettle which was boiling its head off.

Roz didn't speak, she couldn't. The hard lump in her chest was dissolving into tears and she was striving not to let them fall. Her tongue flickered out to moisten her dry lips.

'Don't *do* that!' he snarled. 'I came down here to beat you to death.' His arms were round her and he kissed her instead, dragging her savagely against him and taking his time about it, and then his hand found the opening in the robe and she shivered with delight at his touch. She knew she shouldn't be like this, that she should be strong and fend him off, remain unmoved, but she could no more stop her involuntary response than she could have stopped the sun in the sky. She slumped in his arm, seduced by the caress of his hand on the smooth skin of her hip, and moaned when he began an insidious exploration of her body.

'What's this?' he demanded thickly as he fingered the collar of the faded old candlewick robe which had started life purple and white but had now faded to a pale petunia and cream. Now that she had stopped resisting, he had both hands free and he slipped the material from her shoulders and nuzzled into the warm flesh at the base of her neck.

'Eve's,' she managed the first word with a gulp, raising a hand to caress the back of his neck. More words came from her lips, although she hardly knew what she was saying. 'I didn't bring anything with me ... I was going ...' Whatever she had been going to do, she didn't say; she couldn't. Charles' mouth was straying from her neck down to her breast and she closed her eyes in ecstasy.

'Don't,' she whispered, not meaning it. Last night she had been cold and alone with a dreadful dead feeling inside her, and now she was alive again, every inch of her sensitive to his touch. 'Charles, no, I want an explanation , , '

He raised his head and looked at her, his eyes

heavy and glazed with desire. 'So do I, but we'll
have them later. There's something much more
important first. Damn you, Roz, do you know
what you did to me last night?' She felt him
shudder against her. 'I went through hell, not
knowing where you were, what you were doing,
and I wanted you—God, how I wanted you! I
couldn't do anything except want. I don't think I
could stand another night like that. I want you
now, so . . .' Roz struggled weakly against him,
knowing that she was lost, that she wasn't strong
enough to deny him as he half carried her into the
hall and paused with one foot on the stairs because
she had renewed her struggles.

'Charles, we can't . . .'

'Why not?' Impatience made his voice ragged.

'It's—it's morning,' she stammered weakly.
'Somebody might come. The telephone . . .'

'Whoever comes can knock and go away again—
and,' he reached over the banisters and took the
receiver from its cradle, 'the phone can't ring! As
for it being morning, what's wrong with that?'

Over her shoulder he eyed her rumpled bed
with disfavour. 'It's a bit narrow, but we'll
manage. Stop wriggling, Roz. I need you, and you
want it as much as I do.'

'It's sluttish!' It was a weak protest.

'Be a slut,' he advised grimly. 'My slut.' His
hands were at the fastening of the robe and he
grinned at her devilishly as the edges fell open.
'Didn't you borrow a nightie as well?'

'N-no,' and her lips parted under his, the robe
fell to the floor unheeded and the springs of the
bed protested against the double burden.

'A narrow bed has its advantages.' Charles turned over on his back and stared at the ceiling. 'And I like making love to you in the daylight. That has an advantage too. I can see your face.'

Roz raised her head from where it was lying on his chest and lifted herself on one elbow to look down on him. He looked different somehow; younger, and the strain which had been on his face had disappeared, to be replaced by an expression of content. It curved his mouth and warmed his eyes. 'What about my face?' she asked in a husky whisper.

Charles put up a hand to stroke the line of her cheek and jaw with a proprietorial finger. 'It's even more beautiful . . . no colour, just a red, red mouth, and you cry a bit, did you know that?' He struggled his arm free from where it was trapped beneath her and held her face between his hands. 'The ghost, Roz; have I finally driven it away? Has it gone at last?'

'Ghost?' She looked down at him wonderingly. 'I haven't any ghost, you know that.'

'Yes, you have.' He was sombre. 'Oh, I know Stephen never had you, but it was your first love, Roz, and first loves are lovely things. There's a sweet nostalgia about them, a spring fever where everything's sunny and warm and the grass is very green. I can forgive you for loving him,' he added magnanimously, 'but I don't want that memory living with us; not to always have you comparing me with him.'

'You tell me if it's gone, Charles.' She looked at him straightly. 'It's your ghost, not mine.'

'No, my dear, your brother-in-law doesn't haunt me.'

'What on earth are you talking about?' She sat up, her indignation making her forget modesty so that she didn't pull the sheet up to cover herself. 'It's you who made all the fuss about Stephen, even when I *told* you he meant nothing—and as for that green grass and spring thing, it wasn't anything of the sort. It was a teenage crush. A few kisses, that's all. I never let him . . . you know that.'

'Oh yes, I know,' he smiled at her reminiscently. 'My frightened virgin—but like I said, and although you deny it, that first love's important. It's the glamorous one, the fairly tale, and you told me you couldn't kill off the memory, couldn't forget it. You said we'd have to learn to live with it, don't you remember?'

Her mind fled back to that morning when they'd driven up to town. She had said that, she could recall every word! Suddenly she grew angry. 'I wasn't talking about *me*!' She grew vehement as she pushed her hair back from her face. 'I was talking about you! You and your Margery!' And as if a dam had burst, the words crowded her lips.

'Now it's my turn to ask what you're talking about.' The content had gone from his face and his eyes were furious under their heavy lids. 'What's Margery got to do with it?'

'What's she got to do with it?' she echoed him furiously. 'That's what I want to know, what I've always wanted to know. I suppose you've some ready explanation for what I saw yesterday—yes, what I *saw*! I'm not relying on gossip, although there's been plenty of that—I stood in the hall and watched you!'

'But you know all about Margery.' Charles rolled over, taking her with him. 'Damn it, she met you in town when you were shopping for the wedding—and *she* had to tell me that, you never mentioned it. She said you'd had a long talk . . .'

'Oh yes,' Roz said bitterly, 'we had a long talk, but all I learned was that she'd known you a long time, that you told her everything and that you were very close. Do you know what I felt like, have you any idea? I thought I could take a mistress provided it wasn't an ongoing thing, that I couldn't take—but I saw you. She was plastered all over you, practically eating you, and after that, you have the nerve to talk to me about Stephen! And you come down here and I let you . . . Let me go, I don't want you ever to touch me again!'

'Yes, you do — and I do — and I'll touch you and have you whenever I want!' Charles was equally angry, 'No, shut up for a minute and listen to me. I'm not sure what you saw, but you've got the wrong idea. I've known Marge a long time, ever since we were kids together in the orphanage—we were no relation, but we sort of adopted each other. I was a bit older and a bit bigger and I looked after her. They encouraged that sort of thing, they said it fostered a family feeling, and that's all Marge was to me, a bit of family.'

'Family!' Roz shrilled. 'You lived with her for

years! That's common knowledge. Everybody knew about it . . .'

'Then everybody knew wrong, you bad-minded little bitch!' His hands were firm on her arms and the weight of his body stopped her threshing attempts to get out of bed. 'She lived in my house, she didn't live *with* me, not ever. I'm not her type.'

'Not your type?' Roz glared up at him with frustration. 'I don't believe it. She lived with you, and what's more, she turned a blind eye to your other women. Yes,' she said it with satisfaction and viciously, 'I know about those as well, I could name every one. All I can say is that your Margery has a very forgiving nature. Each time you'd finished with your tomcat on the tiles act, she took you back. You should have married her,' the last words came out on a sob.

'Roz,' the hard grip on her arms relaxed, but his weight still held her, 'I could strangle you! Lie still!' as she started to wriggle furiously. 'I'll tell you about Marge and you'll listen, because I'll only tell you the once. Are you going to listen?'

'I can't do much else,' she muttered sulkily.

'Like I said, Marge and I were together in the orphanage. She was a funny little thing and she used to come running to me when she'd hurt herself or when one of the big boys she admired so much had pulled her hair or pushed her over.'

'For comfort, I suppose?' There was a world of sarcasm in her voice.

'Yes, for comfort. She was only about four.

Who did you run to' for comfort, Roz—your
mother? Marge and I weren't so lucky, remember. But as soon as she was better, off she
went again. She had a thing about big, blond
types like your brother-in-law and she's a rotten
picker, they either let her down or knock her
about.'

'She lived with you for five years.' Roz refused
to be mollified. ·

'Correction, darling,' his hand slid to her waist
and held it firmly, 'she lived in my house, to our
mutual advantage.'

'That's what I said,' she interrupted, 'only I
wasn't so mealy-mouthed about . . .'

'Be quiet!' His mouth found hers and cut off
the interruption. 'I said I'll only explain once. She
left the orphanage the same year I did and went
to work in an office, rooming with some other
girls. Everything went well for a couple of years,
she found a man, another big blond, and eventually they were married. He was in the Merchant
Navy and the jealous type. When he came home,
he used to beat her up to make her confess who
she'd been having while he was away. It got to
the stage where she was telling him anything to
stop being knocked about, and she got out and
filed for a divorce. I fixed up another job for her
in another office and I thought she'd learned her
lesson—but no, the boss in the office was just
her type and,' his lips twisted in derision, 'he had
an advantage. He had a wife who didn't understand him.'

'Like I don't understand you!'

'Don't interrupt,' and Charles placed his hand

over her mouth to enforce the command.
'Everything was quiet, I was busy trying to break
into the big time; I didn't have much time to spare
for anybody, and while this was going on, Marge
had let the fellow move her into a nice little flat
which he shared with her during the week. At
weekends, he went home to his wife and family.
He told her that he was going to get a divorce
and marry her, and Marge believed him. She
went on believing him for years, apparently he
was very plausible, until Marge discovered she
was going to have a baby and then, goodbye lover
boy! He was back with his wife and an aura of
domestic felicity within the hour. Are you still
listening?' he asked with a searching look at her
face.

'Mmm, I can't do anything else.' She was still
mutinous.

'Marge phoned me when she came out of hospital. She'd lost the baby, she was ill, too ill to
work, she owed a month's rent on the flat and the
landlady was threatening to turn her out and she
was flat broke, so I went round straight away and
collected her and her things and brought her back
to my place.'

'And the mutual advantage?' Roz wasn't convinced.

Charles chuckled reminiscently. 'I'd been doing
some shots of a new model when the phone rang;
she was only a young girl, a beauty queen or
something, and she was full of ambition. I
finished off the shots and grabbed my coat, telling her to let herself out and slam the door
behind her. When I got back with Marge, I took

her into my bedroom to show her where she could sleep for the night. I was going to doss down on the divan in the lounge, and there was the little ...' he choked back an uncomplimentary epithet, substituting 'beauty queen' in its stead.

'In your bed.' Roz was overcome by a wild desire to giggle.

'Not in it, on it, and without a stitch on. Somebody had told her that the way to success was via the photographer's bed. I got out quickly and left Marge to deal with the girl.'

'Coward!' This time the giggle would not be stifled.

'Maybe,' he was grim, 'but I was taking no chances. Marge stayed on as secretary-cum-chaperon, it was safer for me that way. There's another fellow in the offing now, but her love life's gone sour on her again. The man's turned out to be another married man with a wife who doesn't understand him. That's why she was crying on my shoulder. But that's enough about Marge, isn't it time we had some breakfast?'

'It's not enough about Marge,' Roz protested. 'Is she going to be crying on your shoulder for the rest of her life?'

'No, my heart, on yours,' he said promptly. 'I'm delegating the responsibility. Next time her love life gets into a knot, *you* shall cope with it. Satisfied?'

'You've never said you love me,' she mourned.

'Love you? Don't be an idiot, Roz. I don't just love you, I adore you. I could exist without you, but it wouldn't be living. I loved you from the moment you came into the studio for the first time. You were perfect, did you know? Hair, skin, face, body, legs; I was so full of lechery, I could hardly talk to you. The way you walked, the way you held your head—I wanted you then, but there were memories, a shadow in your eyes. You didn't really see me, you were lost in a sad little dream. I tried, you know I tried—but you wouldn't.' He kissed her again and her heart leapt to meet the beat of his. 'The last time you came, the shadow was deeper. I thought it was time you stopped grieving over the past, so I made a play for you in earnest. The response was so much more than I'd hoped for!'

'And you followed me down here, you lied, you cheated . . . How did you know I'd be here this time?'

'I didn't, but with hindsight, there wasn't anywhere else you could be. I looked in the bureau when I couldn't find you, you'd left your wallet and your cheque book behind. When your sister phoned, I thought it was the police or a hospital . . .'

'Eve phoned . . .'

'. . . From New York at two o'clock this morning. She'd forgotten the time lag, she thought she'd catch us just after dinner. I asked her where you'd go and she said "Home, of course". Is this still home to you, Roz?'

'No,' her face became grave and her eyes misted, 'home's where you are.'

'And I need feeding,' Charles prompted gently. 'It's nearly noon. Don't you want anything?'

'I want a baby,' she said dreamily. 'I don't want to wait for years and years.'

Charles threw back the duvet and slid out of bed and she watched him pull his pants up over his lean hips. He leaned down and kissed her mouth. 'I'll redouble my efforts,' he promised. 'After I've been fed!'

Harlequin® Plus

A CLASSIC BRITISH DISH

Charles serves Roz a steak-and-kidney pie with an aroma that makes Roz's mouth water. This classic dish is one you can use to make mouths water, too!

1 veal kidney	6 medium carrots, peeled & sliced
1 lb. round steak	
1 cup flour	1 large onion, coarsely chopped
1 tsp. rosemary	
1 tsp. thyme	2 stalks celery, coarsely chopped
1 tsp. oregano	
½ tsp. salt	1 large casserole dish with lid
¼ tsp. garlic powder	
pepper to taste	1½ cups pastry
2 tbsp. vegetable oil	1 "pie bird"
2½ cups beef stock	pastry brush
(may be bouillon cubes)	milk

Cut out hard white core of kidney, then thoroughly wash remainder in cold water and slice into bite-sized pieces. Cut steak into 1-inch cubes. Put flour and next six ingredients into plastic bag. Add kidney and steak, and shake to coat thoroughly. In oil in large, medium-hot frying pan, brown kidney and steak. Remove meat and add beef stock to pan. Bring to boil, stirring constantly. Remove from heat.

Place kidney, steak, carrots, onion, celery and stock in casserole. Cover and cook in preheated 350°F (175°C) oven for 2½ hours. Remove and cool until casserole is just warm to touch.

Roll out pastry on floured board to approximate size of top of casserole dish. Place "pie bird" in center of casserole, wet rim of dish with water, then place pastry over top, making sure it reaches the rim. Trim excess, then pinch edge of pastry to rim. Cut an X in pastry to allow pie bird's "beak" to protrude. Brush pastry lightly with milk. Bake at 475°F (245°C) for 15 minutes. Turn down to 350°F (175°C) and bake 30 minutes more. Serves 4 to 6.

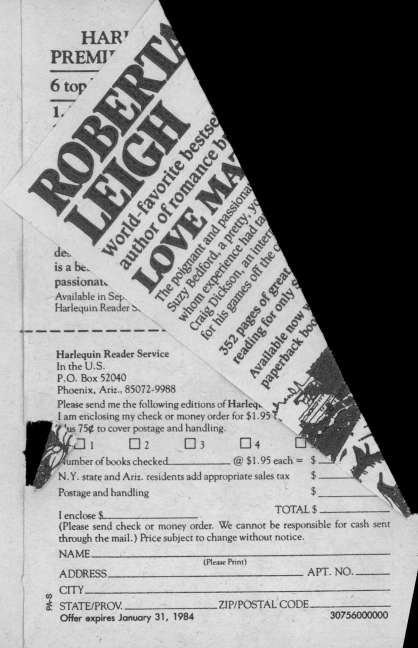

'I want a baby,' she said dreamily. 'I don't want to wait for years and years.'

Charles threw back the duvet and slid out of bed and she watched him pull his pants up over his lean hips. He leaned down and kissed her mouth. 'I'll redouble my efforts,' he promised. 'After I've been fed!'

A CLASSIC BRITISH DISH

Charles serves Roz a steak-and-kidney pie with an aroma that makes Roz's mouth water. This classic dish is one you can use to make mouths water, too!

1 veal kidney	6 medium carrots,
1 lb. round steak	peeled & sliced
1 cup flour	1 large onion,
1 tsp. rosemary	coarsely chopped
1 tsp. thyme	2 stalks celery,
1 tsp. oregano	coarsely chopped
½ tsp. salt	1 large casserole
¼ tsp. garlic powder	dish with lid
pepper to taste	1½ cups pastry
2 tbsp. vegetable oil	1 "pie bird"
2½ cups beef stock	pastry brush
(may be bouillon cubes)	milk

Cut out hard white core of kidney, then thoroughly wash remainder in cold water and slice into bite-sized pieces. Cut steak into 1-inch cubes. Put flour and next six ingredients into plastic bag. Add kidney and steak, and shake to coat thoroughly. In oil in large, medium-hot frying pan, brown kidney and steak. Remove meat and add beef stock to pan. Bring to boil, stirring constantly. Remove from heat.

Place kidney, steak, carrots, onion, celery and stock in casserole. Cover and cook in preheated 350°F (175°C) oven for 2½ hours. Remove and cool until casserole is just warm to touch.

Roll out pastry on floured board to approximate size of top of casserole dish. Place "pie bird" in center of casserole, wet rim of dish with water, then place pastry over top, making sure it reaches the rim. Trim excess, then pinch edge of pastry to rim. Cut an X in pastry to allow pie bird's "beak" to protrude. Brush pastry lightly with milk. Bake at 475°F (245°C) for 15 minutes. Turn down to 350°F (175°C) and bake 30 minutes more. Serves 4 to 6.

HARLEQUIN
PREMIERE AUTHOR EDITIONS

6 top Harlequin authors — 6 of their best books!

1. JANET DAILEY Giant of Mesabi

2. CHARLOTTE LAMB Dark Master

3. ROBERTA LEIGH Heart of the Lion

4. ANNE MATHER Legacy of the Past

5. ANNE WEALE Stowaway

6. VIOLET WINSPEAR The Burning Sands

Harlequin is proud to offer these 6 exciting romance novels by
6 of our most popular authors. In brand-new beautifully
designed covers, each Harlequin Premiere Author Edition
is a bestselling love story—a contemporary, compelling and
passionate read to remember!

Available in September wherever paperback books are sold, or through
Harlequin Reader Service. Simply complete and mail the coupon below.

- -

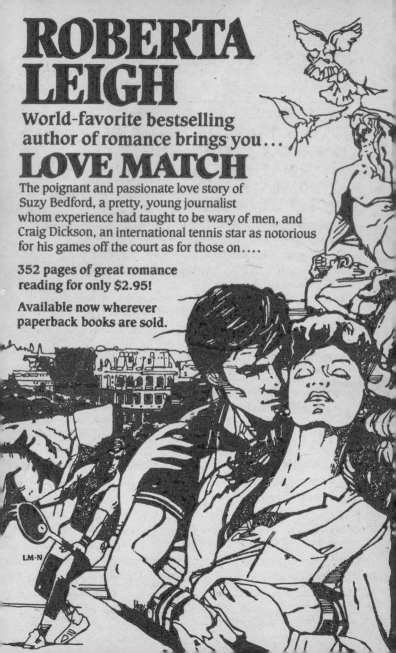